Upside Down

Copyright 2013 by Corey Wellman

Published by Black Water Publication

Printed in the United States of America
2014

Dedication

To my other half who without this wouldn't be possible. You're not only my motivation, you're the reason that I dream—Amina Wellman...

Location; Nashville, TN

Eastside of the jungle,

Nobody but him and his mother,

Father gone, crack is a role model and you
wonder!!!

PROLOGUE

Justus got out of his all black Range Rover and approached the house, AR15 in hand like a soldier. He didn't bother knocking. If Low was watching his surveillance cameras he'd seen him coming, if not he would die like Scarface. Justus slammed his boot against the door successfully bending the hinges back. He was met by Debbie, Low Don's chocolate stallion. In her hand was a small caliber pistol, she aimed at Justus and fired missing his head by inches. He squeezed, "Tat, tat, tat, tat!" The blast from the AR15 chopped her in half and shells poured on the floor like change. Justus made his way up stairs slowly checking every room he passed. There was no sign of Low. Then he spotted it; a back window open, curtains blowing in the breeze...

CHAPTER 1

COME HELL OR HOT WATER!!!

"Justus, Justus! Get up boy, damn! You ain't got all day, it's 8:15. That bus will be here any minute and you're up in here sleep. Are you out of your damn mind? Your teacher's already calling me about you done missed too many days of school anyway. What the hell you trying to do send me to jail? I ain't going to jail for you," Pam said.

"Momma, I ain't sleep. I'm looking for my shoes," Justus said as he stood up and stretched lazily.

"Well, hurry up and I hope you haven't torn that room up. I came in there yesterday and it looked like Jurassic park. Dirt all on the floor...what the hell you growing in there?" Pam said as she sat on the couch drinking her morning cup of coffee. Nothing like the fresh taste of caffeine to get a day started.

Justus walked back and forth in his room as if trying to remember something he had forgotten, a trick that never seemed to work. He massaged his temples.

"She always nagging. I be glad when I get my own spot," he thought to himself.

He reached into his closet, on the right side deep in a corner sat a shoe box next to an old cracked picture of his father. In the picture he sported a black trench coat and if you looked closely it was clear that his hand held a gun.

"Money, I gotta have it. Show me the loot, I'll grab it," Justus rapped to himself as he removed an all-black 40 caliber Smith and Wesson from the box then placed it in his waist band, one of the reasons that he liked baggy shirts.

Justus was just fifteen years old, but he stuck to the code of the streets: "better with it than without it." He learned from his father's mistakes. His father learned from experience after being shot ten times. "Never get caught slipping," he could still hear him say. He respected his father to the utmost. Sometimes he would appear in his dreams and they would have a conversation, even share a laugh, although he never was there in reality. He left when Justus was only eight years old and was serving a twenty year bid up north for chasing that paper...so much for a role model.

Justus resembled his father in many ways. They were both tall. At fifteen years old Justus was 6'3, 280 pounds, nice build, and fast on his feet. He wore a bald head just like his dad, even talked like him. His mother use to tell him all the time, "Boy, you're just like your damn daddy...sometimes it scares me."

Justus grabbed his coat off the back of a chair and quickly headed for the door.

"No fighting and pay attention, Justus. I don't need you failing...do you hear me? You're going to be somebody if it kills me...I'm going to see you walk across that stage," Pam said.

"Yea mom I hear you," then the door slammed.

Justus really never thought about graduating. He looked at school kind of like a job. Something you had to do. Pam was proud of her son. They had been through so much. She had struggled so hard to raise him right, even though they were by themselves in the worst part of Nashville; the eastside.

Pam was 35 years old and didn't look a day over it; dark skin, 5'5, and 165 pounds. In high school they called her Chocolate Chip because of her dark complexion. The name Chip sort of stuck with her.

Chip loved Justus with all of her soul and would do anything it took to see him succeed. He was her baby, her only child whom she would die for.

On Fridays, it seemed like school never ended, the anticipation of going home seemed more intense on Fridays. Time had a funny way of doing that. If you're waiting on something it takes forever, pay no attention and it'll sneak up on you and you'll find yourself unprepared. The fifth period math teacher, Mr. Smith, wasn't making it any better and besides, Justus hated math. It was his worst subject. He literally hid in the back of the class trying to not get called on.

"Hey Tina," Justus whispered. "Tina, I know you hear me calling you, cute face. What's the answer to number five? I'm stuck," he said pencil tapping his paper impatiently.

Tina Dunlap was your average hood rat; blue hair, black lipstick, foul mouth and really not cute at all, but the nickname "Cute Face" was a joke and she liked it. In her own eyes she really was cute and bet nobody could tell her different.

"What stupid? Don't tell me that your smart ass don't know the answer," Tina said snapping her neck like the typical drama queen.

"Why you got to diss your boy like that? Can we have one day of peace? You know that you love a nigga like me anyway," Justus said leaning back in his chair, ego swagging.

"Nigga please, I love when you quiet, which is barely ever," Tina said.

A few students began to laugh. A boy named Corey Lanear a.k.a. Foot, the ring leader of the class clowns and Go Hard Mafia Gang spoke up and repeated after Tina, "Love when you quiet." Then he took his hand, made the shape of a gun and pointed it at Justus, fired, then blew the tip of his finger like he was cooling the barrel and laughed turning back to his homeboy.

Foot had a reputation for being ruthless. The streets spoke loud when it came to his dirt. He was only seventeen years old and already he had shot seven people and beat a few others unconscious. He hardly ever came to school and when he did it was trouble. Black and bigger than an ape, he was known for putting the smack down and bulling his way around.

"Man, did you see what that Foot nigga just did?" Brick whispered to Justus. "Seems like he got something on his mind, he'll make a nigga get at him...I ain't feeling that," he said.

Brick was no stranger to danger, he'd been in more fights than Ali. Win, lose, or draw only to fight again. Brick was sixteen, tall, pigeon-toed, light skin, and slim with dreams of becoming the next 50cent, although he was not your average guy in a video.

Brick and Justus had been friends since they were little. Justus' mom used to keep Brick on the weekends when Brick's mom worked late. They were as close as brothers. He got the nickname, "Brick" a few years back for smashing a dude's head in with a huge rock outside of the movie theater.

"Yea, I saw that fool. I guess he shucking for Tina. Nigga know he don't want it. I'm 'bout tired of that nigga anyway. I think he still trippin' off that Brigit broad," Justus said laughing.

"Doody Brigit," Brick said.

"Doody booty Brigit," said Justus and turned his nose up, as if she had just walked into the room and he could smell her. Although she didn't really stink, she was a slut and well on her way to a house full of kids, incurable diseases, and public housing.

"But you ain't never messed with no Brigit," said Brick.

"I know...I tried to tell that fool. I guess he didn't believe me, he got me confused with you," they laughed.

Pam sat at the kitchen table with a headache out of this world. There were some cravings that caffeine just couldn't satisfy. She couldn't believe what was happening to her, she was falling apart. Ever since Ricky had introduced her to cocaine, she had been crumbling to pieces. Her life had suddenly taken a turn for the worse and Justus was out of control, she knew that he owned a gun. She had found it one day while she was snooping in his room looking for change. "What the hell is he doing with a gun," she wondered, but refused to confront him because then he'd know she'd been snooping.

What would he do if he found out about her addiction? How long could she hide it if everything done in the dark comes to light? Her hands were shaking terribly, she needed a hit. Picking up her purse she emptied all the contents on the kitchen table. Just as she had expected: not a penny to her name. She picked up the phone and dialed a number quickly and waited for an answer. After the fourth ring a raspy voice answered.

"Hello?"

"Hello, may I speak to Ricky," Pam said.

Her heart began to race and she could feel a tiny bead of sweat run down her cheek.

"Who's calling?" Ricky said.

"Oh, this is Pam. Ricky?"

"Hey Pam, baby. What's up? Long time no hear. I was just thinking about you yesterday...What's good? How can I help you?" he said.

"Umm, look Ricky. My check didn't come today. I know that I owe you, but you know that I'm good for it...I need a gram," said Pam.

"You cooking ham! I don't eat no pork baby, but I'll be there in a minute," and the phone went dead.

Foot and his homeboy, Puff, sat backed in the driveway of Brigit's house, listening to Lil Wayne's new mix tape in Foot's new Charger (one of his dream cars, canary yellow humming bird on 24's, he called it).

"Who said crime didn't pay? Nigga pass that blunt, you can only get so high. I done sat here and watched you smoke half the stick. I guess you think I'm gonna twist another one, nigga you better roll that shit up," Foot said.

Puff began to choke then inhaled the smoke in through his nose and blew out slowly smiling, looking out the window bobbing his head. He passed the blunt to Foot.

"Guess what you look like nigga?" Puff said.

"What do I look like?" Foot asked.

"Nigga, you look like a monkey," Puff said and then began to laugh. Puff was a big fat nigga who could pass for the entertainer 8 Ball, but he kept his hair cut low. Foot laughed, too.

"Well, I guess I could pass for a monkey, nigga with all this red monkey on my back. Nigga, you heard Jeezy. 'These eight hunneds sagging on these apes'...fool you're still wearing Girbauds, my lil' brother wouldn't even put them on," Foot said.

"That's because your lil' brother broke nigga and he ain't got no taste. You liable to see him in some biker shorts with his soft ass," Puff began to laugh, but was cut short by a quick jab to his mouth. His bottom lip split open and began to bleed. He covered his head afraid that Foot would strike him again.

"Watch your mouth fool. Who do you think you're talking to? Don't make me mad," Foot said.

"Man, you know I'm just playing bruh. You trippin'," said Puff wiping blood on his shirt.

"Find another way to play." Foot put the car in drive and slowly crept out from Brigit's drive way. He turned right on to Lischey Avenue and sped up with one hand gripping the wood and the other scanning the CD changer. He stopped when he came to Trick Daddy's CD and began to sing along.

"In this life I've lived I done seen niggas killed." The yellow charger zoomed through traffic as if it were a bee.

Foot looked over at Puff and said, "Man, Brigit is starting to get on my nerves. I'm tired of her playing these mind games. I'm thinking about moving on," he said.

"Ohhh, so that's what this is about? Nigga done hit me in the mouth because he's mad at Brigit. Nigga needs to be hitting Justus in the mouth because he's the one hitting it not me," Puff said.

"Naw, I hit you in the mouth because you're always running your mouth, you don't know when to shut up. I was hoping that it would have taught you a lesson, but I see you're still having problems," Foot said.

Suddenly a cherry red F150 with limo tints pulled up beside Foot's charger. The window rolled down exposing an AK47 and two men in ski mask. The chopper roared like an angry lion, a burst from the AK sent glass flying through the car. Puff yelled. Foot yanked the steering wheel left and mashed on the brake coming to a sudden stop, rims still spinning.....

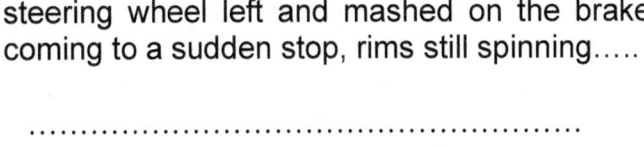

Monday afternoon, fifth period math teacher, Mr. Smith, who was on his fourth cup of coffee, could hardly sit down. He had called almost each and every one of his students up to the board to solve a problem.

"Ok class, this next one is a no brainer: E + square = what, Brad?"

Brad Fletcher was Brick's government name.

"I don't know," Brick said.

"What do you mean you 'don't know'? Have you not being paying attention?" Mr. Smith said angrily.

Brick was fumbling with his button on his shirt nervously.

"Yea, I was paying attention, but I just can't remember for some reason," Brick said.

"Yea, I bet you can't remember. Maybe if you could stop talking to Mr. Abernathy you would know something," Mr. Smith said. The class began to laugh. Brick lowered his head wishing that he could disappear. Mr. Smith called on someone else so Brick and Justus continued to talk.

"Man you heard what happen to your boys?" Brick said.

"Who dat?" asked Justus.

"What! Foot and that nigga Puff? Don't tell me that you ain't heard, it's all around the school," Brick said.

"Naw, I ain't heard nothing...what happen to them suckas?" asked Justus.

"Man, I overheard Brigit telling Lil' Mommy that some niggas tried to kill him. Said something about they sprayed his Charger up and shot Puff in the face...Puff in ICU," Brick said.

"Fool you playing...What about Foot?" Justus said.

"Not a scratch on him. That fool supposed to be laying low on some Machiavelli shit. Say he 'bout to 'Hell Mary' some niggas. We better play it safe too, we might be on his list," Brick said.

"Who they saying did it?" said Justus.

"Nobody know, that's what I'm saying. Say they had masks on and it was two niggas though," Brick said.

Justus started to massage his temples, thinking hard. He knew it was a matter of time before names started to be tossed around, and + his name would come up. And if that were to happen, all hell would break loose and he needed to be ready. Just the thought of beef made his palms sweat. He readjusted the 40 caliber on his hip and glanced around the class.

"Well, I guess this is it...I'm out this piece, meet me at my house in an hour," Justus said.

"No doubt," Brick said. "Oh yea, bruh...."

"What's up?" Justus asked.

"Be safe," Brick said.

CHAPTER 2

FISH SCALES!!!

(A few years later)

Foot and his man, Marrelle McClenton a.k.a. Cain, sat at a table negotiating prices. Cain, a spokesperson for Lamaine Ware a.k.a. Low Don, was trafficking dope from state to state. He liked fast money, fast cars and had enough of both. Even though he was the middle man. He was satisfied with his position in the game and was loyal to Low Don.

Cain sat back reclining in a lazy boy chair with a black Louis Vuitton briefcase sitting in front of him on the table. He opened the briefcase and begun removing bricks of white powder and lining them up on the table. Foot was conversing on his cell phone with one of his workers. "No, no, no, Bobby I can't do that baby. You know that you're my nigga, but this work high, straight fish scales baby. None of that off white that we've been having...it's starting to dry up too. Ain't no telling when I'm going to get some more," Foot said.

Foot was popping game and Bobby was eating it up. The truth was, Low Don didn't believe in droughts. He was connected and the

Columbians made sure he had more than enough.

"Ok nigga," Bobby said.

"Same place, but make sure you bake that bread right. I don't have time to be recooking no dough. You was short last time," Foot said.

"The bread baked fool. It's all there," Bobby said,

"That's what I'm talking about...that's why I like you. I can trust you to do things right," Foot said stroking Bobby's ego. He stood up from the table and walked over to a window looking out over the city then he looked down and smiled.

"Speaking of doing things right, what's the static on that other issue that I had you looking into? I haven't been able to sleep all night," Foot said.

"Still no news, boss. Me and the team got our ears to the streets, we ain't heard nothing and we're looking hard," said Bobby.

"Look harder, somebody knows something. Niggas talk too much to keep hush. I want them niggas dead," Foot said. Then he walked away from the window and sat back in his chair.

"And they will be. As a matter of fact some of the homeboys out setting examples right now as we speak. The word is out: don't nobody fuck with the mafia," Bobby said.

"Same time," Foot said and pushed the end button on his cell disconnecting the call. Cain didn't know what the hell was going on, but from the sounds of it somebody had messed up.

"What's troubling you my friend?" Cain asked feeling the Ecstasy pill kick in. His mouth began to rock and he was sweating, trying not to chew his tongue off.

"Excuse me, I kind of lost it...some niggas tried to off me and my homeboy a few years ago and the doctors don't expect him to live much longer. His health is deteriorating. I got the news yesterday. They are considering taking him off the machine. His coma has destroyed his brain. The shit is eating at me and revenge is long overdue. Somebody got to pay. But back to business. You tell Low that I said two days and as always I appreciate it," Foot said,

"No problem," Cain said putting his shades on and heading out the door.

The black Lexis LS was a site to see, no doubt eye candy for all those who watched.

Lambo doors and the twenty-two inch chrome Ashanti's made it look as though the car was crawling.

Fat Tony, a rival of Go Hard Mafia, pulled over at the AM PM market for gas feeling like a super star. He pulled in with his door up, dressed to impress; twenty one hundred dollar jogging suit, matching air force ones, chain hanging low with a medallion that read, 'Rich'... truly a work of art. He parked and stepped out the Lexis leaving the doors up, never noticing the white Caprice pulling in beside him. The driver of the Chevy yelled, "Hey Tony, I need to holla at cha."

Tony turned around and said, "What's up?" only to find himself starring down the barrel of a pump. "That Mafias what's up...which one of your punk ass homeboys tried to kill my niggas?" Darrel said.

Darrel Wallace a.k.a. Lil' Darrel was a foot soldier for the Mafia and loved to put in work. He had dropped more niggas than a cannon. One time he drowned a whole family in the bathtub in a robbery that went terribly wrong and left with nothing but four more bodies to his name. He had no problem pulling the trigger and was good at it. He had brought death to quite a few people. Tony's eyes opened wide and his mouth dropped, he couldn't believe this was happening to him. So many thoughts were running through his mind, the fear of being shot to death was enough to kill him. He imagined the burning sensation of hot led and the terrible agony a bullet ripping through his flesh might cause.

Where in the hell did this nigga come from? Had he been followed?...Who is this nigga?...What in the hell is he talking about?...How in the hell does he know me? Tony wanted to strike out running but had seen Boys In the Hood enough to know that could cause him death immediately. He considered screaming, but decided to hold on to his pride. He wasn't ready to die, he was only twenty two and besides where would he run to? He decided to try to talk his way out of it. "If it's money you want man, you can have it...I got plenty of it. Just let me make a phone call and that shit will pull up in trucks...take my chain, it's platinum or my car. Don't shoot me, man. I ain't never shot nobody," Tony said voice trembling,

"I'll ask you again and you better tell me something or I'ma pump you like some Reeboks," Darrel said aiming the pump at Tony's head laughing.

"Look, I swear," said Tony with tears in his eyes, and with his last strength he took off. "BOOM!" the pump exploded his head like a hot air balloon sending skull fragments and brains everywhere. The vibration of the gage shook Darrel's body like an earthquake. A second shot sent Tony's body flying in the air as if he were a frisbee. A lady who had witnessed the shooting took cover behind a gas pump screaming for dear life. Darrel turned and aimed at the gas pumps and fired. "BOOM!" fire leaked from the pumps as they tumbled over exploding and at the same time killing the lady instantly in broad daylight. The rest is history. The white caprice disappeared in traffic as if it never existed.

No   face......................   no   case.

CHAPTER 3

SAVAGE LOVER!!!

The parking lot of Red Lobster was packed. There was hardly any place to park. Brick decided to take his girlfriend, Shawn Lillard, out. After all that fussing she had did he still had to eat so that didn't stop him from taking her out. When they approached the door Shawn started again with her hands on her hips.

"Nigga, I just know that you're going to be a real man...try opening the door sometimes," she said.

"I am a real man, that's why you ain't at Burger King," said Brick.

"Whatever," Shawn said, angrily yanking the door open. "You make me so sick."

Brick smiled as they walked in and the waiter directed them to a table. Shawn sat down by the window.

"You know Brick, I don't know how to take you, sometimes you're so sweet and other times you're mean as hell."

"Naw baby, that's where you're wrong. I ain't never mean. I'm just me...I be having a lot on my mind, you know these streets wicked," he said.

"Yea, but that don't mean that you have to take it out on me. I'm suppose to be the one you can talk to," Shawn said reaching across the table taking Brick's hand in hers. She massaged them gently.

"But you're always talking like your ears don't work. All that I ask you to do is hold me down," Brick said.

"And I do Brick, but all that I ask you to do is hold me!" Shawn was starting to get upset and she was raising her voice. "Do you even know the last time that you touched me?" Shawn asked.

"Is that what this is about? You want a nigga to touch you? I got a million things on my mind other than sex. It ain't what drives me. I'm out here trying to get it. School don't cut it, I gave up on basketball a long time ago. I'm really like fuck school, it's a waste of time."

"So what drives you? Money? Because that's all you want to do is hang in them streets and sell that shit," she said.

"You don't know what a nigga doing in these streets, you act like I like it out here. You don't know what I go through and you don't care. It's like you don't care because you're in it for yourself. You think it's all about you, but it's not," removing his hands from Shawn's. He took a sip of water that the waiter had placed on the table.

"I never said it was all about me," Shawn said.

"You don't have to say...you don't have to, your action shows it. You're spoiled and you think everything supposed to go Shawn's way or the highway. You're cute baby, but understand this: it ain't all about looks," Brick said then waved his hands up signaling for the waiter. A different guy with dreadlocks, who kind of favored the old Buster Rhymes, came over to serve them. He spoke with a Jamaican accent and kept his eyes on Brick not wanting to be rude, but Shawn was truly a work of art; caramel color skin, slanted eyes, curves in all the right places.

"Yea mon...What can I help you with this evening?" the waiter asked.

Brick took a quick glance over the menu smiling. He looked up at the waiter and said, "Well, you can start by keeping your damn eyes off my woman. I got a 45 in my draws, the car I'm in is a rental, I'm parked by the door and I got some shit on my chest I've been needing to get off anyway. Now, for your rudeness, free shrimp pasta for my lady, and free shrimp scampi for me, sweet tea to drink and hold the ice," Brick said leaning back exposing the handle of his ruga.

"Yea mon," the waiter said and headed for the kitchen promptly.

"Boy you crazy, you just scared the hell out of that man. He's probably gone to get the police. 'Free shrimp pasta for my lady', boy you're a savage.

"But you love me," Brick said.

"Of course I do," Shawn said bending over the table and kissing Brick softly on his forehead.

"So that makes you a savage lover," Brick responded.

"Sounds good to me," she said.

"Me too!" Brick said. They began to laugh. Looks like the night won't be so bad after all.

. . . .

"Knock! Knock! Knock!"

"Who is it?" Pam said, as she sat in the living room watching, The Young and the

Restless. She hated when someone interrupted her stories. She started not to answer the damn door, but the knocking continued.

"Stop beating on my damn door...who is it?" Pam said jumping up and sliding into her flip-flops. She peeped through the peephole and saw that it was Brick then she opened the door.

"Hey momma, is Justus in? I tried calling his cell, but no answer. I figured that his battery must be dead so I just came on ova."

"Boy you making me miss my darn Young and the Restless," Pam said then hurried back over to the couch. "Yea he's back there. I guess you can go on back there. Boy quit acting like you don't know where you at...Justus you got company!" Pam hollered and zoned back out into the T.V. It wasn't the plasma that she dreamed of, never the less, it was nice.

Brick walked back to Justus' room and opened the door. He almost fainted when he saw Justus standing in the middle of the floor aiming a Mac10 with a silencer directly at him. The scene was straight out of a movie.

"It's me, what the hell you doing bruh?" Brick said trying to catch his breath. The sight of the Mac10 made him dizzy. He was still trying to figure out what was going on.

"Company is not always welcome, ain't that right Violent?" Justus said to his all black Persian cat as he lowered the gun.

Violent had been with Justus since he was a kitten. Justus found him in the alley with a broken leg. Since then they had been best friends. Violent jumped up on Justus' shoulder and starred at Brick wickedly.

"I didn't know who the hell you were busting through the door like that. Lately a nigga been spooked. I almost popped my own shadow yesterday. I'm not trying to let no nigga steal on me, My pops wouldn't understand that shit. You're lucky that I ain't no pussy nigga, or right now you'd be Swiss cheese," Justus laughed.

"I know," Brick said reaching for a joy stick to the X box 360.

"What that Madden talking about doe, nigga?" Brick said

"You couldn't beat me on your best day boy," Justus said.

"Bet something den fool. I got the Titans."

"Aww hell naw. I know you ain't gonna bet me wit' no Titans, they can't even win in real life," said Justus.

They played a couple of games and Justus punished Brick in silence.

"This is your third game losing bruh. You're lucky I ain't no gambler or you would be broke by now," Justus said.

"Aww you ain't just killing me bruh, give me my props," Brick said.

"Props for what, being a loser? I just smashed you."

"Run it back," said Brick.

"Maybe later, right now I got something else I want to show you. Close your eyes," Justus said then went and stood by the closet.

"Hell naw, I ain't closing my eyes. Nigga you done did enough shocking me for one day. What the hell you got in the closet, a body?" Brick asked.

"Naw nigga, not in my closet. Who you think I am, Jeffery Dommer?" Justus said.

"Is it Brigit?" asked Brick.

"Hell naw, if it is I'm shooting her...so you got jokes, today. I'ma start calling you Bozo the clown," Justus said.

"Ok," Brick said closing his eyes. Justus opened the closet and removed a sack that looked like a drycleaner bag on a hanger. He passed it to Brick.

"This is for you. I hope you like it. They didn't have red so I got you green. Try it on," said Justus.

"Aww hell, my nigga done bought me clothes. What you trying to say I look dirty?" Brick laughed then unzipped the bag revealing a bullet proof vest.

"Man, where in the hell did you get this? I've been wanting one of these for a long time," Brick said.

"Now you got one just like mine, I bought two. Fatso gave me a deal. You know you can buy a bomb from that nigga? Put it on and as much as possible keep it on. I bought us these for a reason. I don't trust them niggas and I ain't been sleeping right since that Foot nigga been playing Machiavelli. I mean he's been my enemy, but at least at school I could watch the nigga, but now he's laying low. He's a threat, and a fool you can't see is dangerous." Justus closed the door and stood facing the mirror. He looked different. So much had changed over the years, the streets had a way of aging you. He had grown up way too fast. If his mom only knew of the things he'd done in the dark.

"You know I was thinking the same thing. What you got in mind?" asked Brick.

"I thought you'd never ask," Justus said rubbing his hands together as if he was anxious. "Well for starts we need a smoke screen, we gotta bring this bitch out. Hit him where it hurts, wait then attack. In other words we're going to pop it off and get this shit out the way. It's on and I can feel it. Ain't no rocking me to sleep. It was no coincidence that Tony got knocked off, he stayed on this same street five houses down from me...it's called the process of elimination. You start at the top of your list and work your way down."

Suddenly the sound of squealing tires caught Justus' attention, followed by the sound of a fully automatic assault rifle and bullets eating their way through bricks, "tat, tat, tat, tat, tat!"

"Get down!" Brick yelled as bullets ripped through the walls. A poster of Malcolm X was cut in half as slugs tore their way through furniture and crumbled drywall.

The thought of someone shooting up Justus' momma's house sent Justus into blind rage. He grabbed the Mac10 off the bed and dashed through the house.

"Momma!" he screamed, no answer. "Momma!" he screamed again. Still no answer.

The shooting finally stopped. He entered the living room and found his mother sitting on the couch with a small line of blood trickling down her face from a nickel size hole in her head.

"Call an ambulance!" he screamed. She was hit.

So Young and So Restless!!!

CHAPTER 4

MR. AR15

Darrel was a lunatic and loved it. He cruised down the street laughing like the maniac he was. His AR15 sat on the seat beside him still smoking, he buckled his seatbelt and focused on driving the speed limit. From a distance you could hear sirens wailing. Darrell was trying not to look suspicious; he sat up in his seat facing forward faking a smile hoping that no one had spotted his Chevy leaving the scene. He grabbed his cell and phoned Bobby.

"Fat boy," he yelled into the phone as Bobby answered.

"What's up fool?" Bobby said.

Darrel began to rap into the phone.

"Who in the hell is gonna stop me, you know murder my hobby, AR get to barking…beat up his body like Rocky."

"Crazy D, what it do baby? I've been looking all over for you. Man I just called your phone…what's popping?" Bobby said.

"That chopper nigga, you know I keep that chopper popping," said Darrel. "Where you at?"

"I'm at the spot, trap or cry. It's jumping, swang by," Bobby said.

"I'm on my way," Darrel said and hung up the phone. He was starting to feel better. Maybe no one had seen him after all.

Five minutes later he was pulling up at Bobby's spot. He laid the AR15 on the floor board of the car and covered it with a towel that he had on the back seat. He noticed Bobby on the porch with a line standing in front of him getting his serve on, dressed in an all black Gucci jogging suit, all black air force ones, diamonds shining.

Darrel parked and jumped out.

"Damn you think you're at da Carter, don't cha? You're trying to new jack the city, 'living just enough for the city'," Darrel begun to sing and snap his fingers.

"Nigga, this easy money, pieces out the front, weight out the back. So what's the word fool?" Bobby said.

"I just tossed Justus spot up. Bounced through and let off 50. You should have seen it. Tat, tat, tat, tat!" Darrel made the sound with his mouth and waved his arms back and forth like Rambo.

"Did you get him?" Bobby asked.

"Man, no nigga could have survived that. When I left it looked like hurricane Katrina had been through there, nothing moving."

"But did you get him?" asked Bobby.

There was a pause. Darrel thought deeply.

"I don't know," he said looking stupid because if he hadn't killed him for sure, Foot would be highly upset and it could cost him his life. Justus was no punk either, which could mean problems, big problems and any heat was not welcomed. Beef is bad for business and there was product that needed to be moved.

"Rule number 1, no room for mistakes. D you're starting to get messy baby, and we can't afford that shit…one slip up in this game could cost you your life and what whip was you driving anyway?" asked Bobby.

"I was in the Chevy," Darrel replied.

"You mean the Chevy that's in my driveway?" Bobby was becoming hysterical, his eyes looked like huge eggs in their sockets.

"Yea," Darrel said.

"Nigga, have you lost your fucking mind? You bring this hot ass car to my spot and I got enough bricks in here to get everybody a life sentence! If you don't get this time bomb out of my yard, I'm going to kill you myself! What are you trying to do?" Bobby had gotten so mad that he was starting to foam at the mouth like a wild dog. "Take that raggedy piece of shit somewhere else and torch it, and buy something else immediately!" Bobby reached into his pocket and pulled out a roll of cash. "Here take this and as a matter of fact get you a truck," Bobby said.

"Ok, bruh...man, I'm sorry. I feel like a fucking idiot," he said.

"Go now nigga!" Bobby ordered and Darrel jogged back to his car. Bobby went back to business as usual.

"Tommy, my main man, my favorite crack head in the world. What you got for me baby?" Tommy was one of the neighborhood smokers. A chubby white guy who kind of favored a chicken. He'd steal anything that wasn't bolted down.

"I need a wake up, nephew. I got something that I know you gone want," Tommy said and removed a VCR from a paper sack. "It's brand

37

new, I got the remote and everything," Tommy said.

"What the hell is that, a VCR? I didn't know they still made them motherfuckers...who in the hell did you get this from? It got to be old, they don't even sell those in the stores no more," Bobby said.

"I got connects. How many you want?" Tommy asked smiling showing his stained crooked teeth.

"I don't want any of them. I don't even know where to find a VCR tape, you couldn't give it to me for free," said Bobby.

"Come on, nephew. I got a bag of tapes at the house. I can run and get them, it won't take me nothing but a second."

"Ah ha! I knew it nigga. You should be ashamed of yourself, you done took this shit from your momma house."

"Naw she has her own VCR, man. This one came out of my room nephew," Tommy said.

"Make up your mind. At first you was connected and now they're coming out of your room...I bet that you got a whole room full of them, don't you?" Bobby said.

"Yea, you better know it," said Tommy.

"Fool, move on man. I ain't got time to be playing with you. Take this and I don't want to see you no more today," Bobby said handing Tommy a fat rock.

"Thanks nephew, good looking out man. I owe you one. Look, if you ever need anybody knocked off you know that you can holla at me, I got you," Tommy said.

Bobby busted out laughing. He couldn't believe what he was hearing. "So now you're a hit man, too?" Bobby asked.

"I didn't say all that, but if the price is right I'll kill a whole room full of niggas, you dig," Tommy said placing the crack rock into his mouth and concealing it under his tongue.

"You out of your damn mind," Bobby said.

....

Watching his mother Pam being lowered into the ground had to be the hardest day of Justus' life. He'd never imagined life without her, it was too much to bear. The world had suddenly seemed to stop, and the pain could only be compared to anger, a rage unconceivable. The people responsible would pay dearly no doubt, even if it meant losing his own life. He swore to that. His revenge would be one talked about for years to come. His heart had turned cold and the beast was let out of the cage.

Luckily Pam had been a firm believer in paying their life insurance, so burying her was no problem, plus Justus stashed every dollar he'd hustled for. He was no fool. He planned on retiring early, damn being an old hustler. She went away in style; gold and white casket, white dress, even white gloves. The money left over Justus donated to charity on behalf of his mother. Yes life had definitely changed. Justus was a man now on his own. Tiffany didn't count. Although she was a good girl, Justus hardly saw her. She was busy with college and lived on campus, they were worlds apart.

It was 98 degrees outside, not a breeze blowing. The heat was so thick you could smell it. The police had been just as hot since Pam's murder. So far they had no suspect, although in news conferences they pled for anybody with any information to come forth. They had turned up empty handed. Detectives had gone door to door seeking anybody who may have seen or heard anything.

Justus refused to talk to the police. He said that he didn't know anything except that his mother was dead. Detective Eric Swanson reassured Justus that he was working extremely hard to solve his mother's case, and would be following up on any leads that they had or received in the future. One way or the other, he would receive justice.

The all black Dodge Magnum had been stolen from a suburban neighborhood in Brentwood. The owner appeared to be wealthy; it was one of five cars in the driveway and was just right for the occasion, it even had a full tank of gas. Justus and Brick were dressed to kill, literally. All black hooded shirts, black kakis, black forces and black leather gloves.

"Man I haven't been over here in a minute. It looks like they have changed some shit on the street... maybe built some new houses or something...if I remember correctly it's the fifth or sixth house on the right and I think she has a gravel driveway, and the mailbox says 'Brigit's World'," Brick said.

Justus drove past the house once checking the scene and checking for nosey neighbors. They turned around at a dead end and headed back down the street on the opposite side. Approaching the house they noticed a blue Taurus pulling in the driveway. Just as Brigit was stepping out of the Taurus and locking the doors, the black Magnum pulled in behind her blocking her exit. Brick and Justus jumped out, with their guns drawn. Brigit opened her mouth as if to scream, but Justus was too quick. His glock 40 slapped her face sending blood squirting from her nose and knocking her off her feet.

"Who's in the house?" Brick asked.

"Nobody's in the house. Please don't kill me. Brick what's going on?" Brigit said.

Justus snatched her to her feet then pushed her toward the house.

"Open the damn door and if Jack jumps out the box it's going to get messy baby," Justus said smiling.

He prayed that Foot was there, perhaps even sleep, that way he could wake him up personally. What a nightmare, his smile deepened. Brigit's hands were shaking terribly. She stuck the key into the door and after a few seconds finally managed to get the key in. Brick rushed in aiming his Tec. He crept through the house like a sniper in training making sure nobody was trying to surprise them, checking the closets, bathroom, and bedrooms.

"It's clear!" Brick said walking back into the living room. Justus shoved Brigit into the kitchen.

"Have a seat, slim. We're going to try to make this less painful as possible so don't worry," Justus said removing a role of duck tape from his pocket.

He began taping Brigit to a chair. Brigit was getting dizzy and her eye had swollen shut. He taped her arms to the back of the chair.

"I haven't done anything... Brick, what's going on?" Brigit asked.

"It's out of my hands, baby. I told you that you should have stayed with me," Brick said jokingly.

"Brigit, sweetheart right now you're in a not so great situation and what I need for you to do is pay very close attention to every word that leaves my mouth. If not this could be very bad for you. Are you following me?" Justus asked.

Brigit nodded her head.

"Good. I knew you were a smart girl. Now, where in the hell is Foot and before you say anything let me tell you what you shouldn't say... One: 'I don't know', this unlucky answer will get you killed immediately," Justus said.

Brigit looked him in the eyes; something was different about his eyes. He seemed to be looking straight through her. She saw death in his eyes. There was no mistaking it, he looked insane.

"I haven't saw him in about a week, we had an argument and he left," Brigit said with tears in her eyes.

"So where did he say he was going?" Justus asked.

"He didn't say, but I think that he may be with Bobby. That's where he always goes when he's mad," Brigit said.

"So where in the hell is Bobby?" Justus asked.

Brigit paused for a second, she was weighing her options. She really didn't want Foot to be hurt, but she really didn't have a choice. If she gave them the wrong address and they knew that she was lying, they would kill her for sure and she had too much to lose.

"405 North 2nd Street. It's a big white house with a green roof...Bobby drives a black Escalade or sometimes a green SS. He usually parks his cars in the back and that's all that I know, I promise, you got to believe me," Brigit pleaded.

"We do," Justus said.

Brigit felt relieved.

"What are you going to do...you're not going to kill me are you? I told you everything I know," Brigit said.

"Of course not. I don't give life or death so whether you survive is totally up to God," Justus said.

Placing his 40 glock up against her eye he squeezed off two shots. Brigit's body violently jerked causing the chair to tumble over spilling brain matter on the floor.

"Damn! She was kind of cute, maybe we should have spared her...Do you think she was telling the truth?" Brick asked.

"I don't know, but let's find out. Eye for an eye."

Upside Down

CHAPTER 5

SUCKER FOR LOVE!!!

Foot was relaxing in the Jacuzzi watching Scarface on the 52 inch plasma screen at the five star hotel in downtown Nashville when his cell phone rang. He answered it on his Bluetooth.

"Hello," he said.

"What's up, bruh?" Bobby said.

"What's up fool? I'm just sitting back popping my toes like a real boss should," Foot replied laughing. "So how's the business?"

"It's great on this end. Actually that's what I was calling to tell you. Your boy Wayne just hit me up and said he needed like twenty girls to come play with him when he land, then I'm through. He should be here in about an hour or so...oh yea I taxed him too," Bobby said.

"You always do nigga, it's in your blood," Foot laughed.

"So, how you feeling? It seems like you done lightened up. How is things at home, have you talked to Brigit?"

"Naw, I ain't talked to her yet, this hoe got me stressed...I was just about to call her though. As a matter of fact I guess that I'll hit her up when I get off the phone with you. I miss her crazy ass."

"I know you do sucka for love ass nigga," Bobby laughed.

Foot disconnected the phone then stepped out of the Jacuzzi, grabbed a towel, dried off, and got dressed. As always, he looked like a million bucks. Today he was wearing red from head to toe and Prada boots. Sitting on the edge of the bed he dialed Brigit's number. No answer, he reached her recorder.

"Hey this is Brigit. Sorry I'm not in, leave a message."

He hung up and redialed the number. Still no answer. He began to get worried. It was unlike Brigit not to answer the phone. Even when she was mad at him she would pick up and at least talk crazy, but not today. He tried calling back blocking his number, but still no answer. He decided to send someone by to check things out so he phoned Bobby back.

"Hey Bobby, look I need somebody to shoot by my house to check on Brigit. I've been calling her and I'm not getting an answer. The phone is going straight to the voicemail and it's full," Foot said.

"No problem. I'll send D by there now. Chill out, I'm sure everything is good. Maybe she sleep," Bobby said.

"Nigga it's 2:00 in the afternoon, she don't take naps. Something is up so get somebody out there now and contact me immediately!" Foot said and hung up the phone. His head had started to hurt so he decided to lie down and rest his eyes.

"Where you at," Bobby yelled to D through the phone? "I need for you to swing by Brigit's now," he said.

"I'm up here by TSU trying to find me a dime. Can it wait? I think I see one now," Darrel was feeling himself. He liked his new truck, a gray Dodge Ram he called it his "low, low".

"No, it can't wait and hurry up Foot is waiting," Bobby said.

"Aight man, I'm on my way," Darrel said then hung up the phone.

"I'll be back ladies," he said to himself and pulled out of the parking lot speeding toward

Brigit's house. He popped in 50 Cent's CD, Get Rich or Die Trying, and let it play.

Pulling up at Brigit's house he noticed her blue Taurus in the driveway, the driver door ajar. He pulled in and parked behind her car checking his 45 colt before he got out of the truck. He approached the door with his gun out.

"Brigit!" he yelled stepping up on the porch. "Brigit, it's Darrel. Brigit!" he yelled again, he noticed that the door was cracked slightly.

"What kind of shit is this? Ain't nobody playing with you girl, I know you hear me calling you, Brigit!" he yelled again, still no answer. Darrel was starting to get paranoid.

"Enough is enough," he kicked the door all the way open waiving his 45.

He stepped in and there she was on the floor bound to a chair with duck tape, half of her head missing and the carpet soaked in blood. The house was starting to stink. The stench of death was so strong that he almost vomited.

"Who in the hell could have did this?" Darrel thought. After a moment or so one person's name seemed to stand out in his head, but it couldn't be. He was dead or wasn't he? He had heard on the news that a person had been killed in a drive-by at his house.

"What the hell is going on?" He ran back out the door to his truck. One thing was for sure; whoever had done this meant business. He dialed Bobby's number while quickly backing out of the driveway.

"What's the word?" Bobby answered.

"Somebody blew her damn head off Bobby...they killed Brigit!" He said screaming into the phone. "I'm sorry, bruh. I'm sorry I failed, please forgive me."

"What in the hell are you talking about, fool?" Bobby said.

"Justus... Justus killed Brigit, bruh. I can feel it, I know it's him."

"I thought you said you handled that, so you didn't get him?"

"I guess not man, but the news said somebody died. I saw it with my own eyes," Darrel said.

"I told you fool, this is what I warned you about. These are the mistakes that get niggas killed. I'm going to check around to see if I can find out something. And if somebody died it shouldn't be hard, so I'mma hit you back, but in the meantime lay low."

"Tell Foot I'm sorry man, I'll find who did this bruh. That's on the mafia," Darrel said.

"Just be cool lil nigga, keep a clear head and stay focused," said Bobby.

"Aight bruh," Darrel said.

Bobby was hysterical. He didn't know how he was going to manage to tell Foot the bad news. It seemed like too much was happening at one time. What ever happen to making money? Niggas was crazy, and the streets were dangerous. You couldn't trust anybody these days.

He called Foot.

"What took you so long? I've been pacing the floor like a mad man...what's up?" said Foot.

"I don't know where to begin...first let me say, Brigit is dead. I sent Darrel by the house. She was there with half her head missing. I'm sorry to have to be the one to tell you this. I know she meant a lot to you." The line went silent. You could hear Foot take a deep breath.

"So who did this?" he asked.

"That's the problem, we don't exactly know, but I got a feeling that it may be Justus or his ghost. Seems like Darrel killed the wrong person," Bobby said.

....

Later that evening as the sun was setting, the eastside seemed peaceful and way too quiet. The black Magnum crept slowly through the alley, stopping at Bobby's back yard.

"Look right there. Bingo. She was telling the truth... there's the black Escalade and the green SS," Brick said excited.

"Do you see any dogs?" Justus asked.

"Not one."

"Good because I don't like dogs."

"I know...you're the only killa I know with a cat," Brick said.

"I'm not a killa, I just kill a lot...what Big Pun say? Ain't that what Big Pun said?" Justus hit Brick softly on the arm laughing.

"I ain't a player, I just crush a lot," Brick corrected.

They parked the stolen Magnum behind a large oak tree and dumpster then hopped out and scaled a small fence. They rushed through the back yard of the house. Through a half open curtain in a small window you could see a figure watching TV. A young lady with long black hair. Brick took the lead slamming his foot into the door sending the door flying off the hinges and wood pieces everywhere, the lady began to scream.

"Crack!" Brick's Tec slamming against her skull silenced her immediately, knocking her unconscious. She passed out on the couch one arm touching the floor, feet dangling similar to a puppet.

Bobby ran out from the kitchen firing a 357 wildly, striking Brick in the chest twice causing him to stagger. The pain opened his mouth wide, as if he'd seen a ghost. Justus then fired his 40 hitting Bobby in the gut. He folded over and collapsed dropping the 357 on the floor wailing like a pig. Brick was in shock but uninjured, the Kevlar ate the slugs. "Thank God for the bullet proof vest," Brick thought.

Bobby was on the ground moaning from all the pain. Justus stood over him smiling, glock aimed at his head.

"Rule one: when a killer's in your house comply or die, you understand Bobby?" Justus yelled.

If Bobby knew Justus at all he would have known he was in serious trouble. Bobby said nothing, which was a mistake. "Crack!" Justus 40 glock slammed into Bobby's head causing blood to ooze.

Again Justus yelled, "When a killer's in your house comply or die...Are you deaf nigga? Where is the money Bobby? Where is the coke? You're running out of time," Justus said placing the barrel on Bobby's temple. Bobby opened his mouth and whispered, "Kill me."

"Now Bobby you don't really mean that," Brick said inserting his Tec 9 into Bobby's mouth. "But we will," Brick replied.

Bobby tried to say something, but could hardly move his tongue due to the gun in his mouth. Brick removed the barrel.

"It's in the kitchen, behind the refrigerator in the wall," Bobby whispered feeling his last strength leaving his body. This wasn't the way he pictured going out, on his back in a pool of his own blood, gun stuffed in his mouth. His whole life flashed before his eyes; his winters spent in Miami, his summers in New York.

Bobby McNeal was originally from New Jersey, but migrated every time he felt the need for a change of scenery. One of the reasons he was able to stay off the police radar for so long. He had been dealing drugs since he was eleven, and at thirty-two he was yet to see the inside of a prison. He called himself lucky, but now it seemed his luck was about to run out. A life time of balling only to die like a bitch.

Justus ran into the kitchen, the refrigerator looked heavy but moved easily.

Voila. There it was.

Justus couldn't believe Bobby was stupid enough to have had this much dope where he laid his head. He was more stupid than he thought.

"Brick! Come take a look at this."

Brick entered the kitchen. His mouth dropped as he watched Justus count the bricks on the floor. He scanned through a duffle bag of money stashed with dope.

"Twenty birds and plenty of stacks...let's get the hell out of here," Brick said leaving the house. Justus turned to Bobby and said, "Today is your lucky day. I would kill you, but for what, and besides you've been so nice to me. Plus you have a job to do. Tell Foot he's a dead man walking. My mother had nothing to do with this beef and now the rules are out the window... and thanks for the raise."

....

Bobby lay hooked to an IV at Centennial Medical Center. His eyes peered around the small but beautifully decorated room. It felt cozy; like home. There were fresh flowers, and balloons sat by a window. Someone had even turned the TV on to the Young and the Restless. He was weak and had lost a lot of blood but he heard the doctors say that he was stable, but he needed rest. He had made it. He had never been so happy to be alive in his life, he had to do better. Maybe even change his life, get a job and fly straight. Maybe it was the medication. All he knew was that he was happy to be breathing. How wonderful it was to still be alive, but because of that bitch Monique he had lost everything. Maybe she was in on it all along, he thought deeply. Naw, she couldn't have been and besides he knew who the robbers were, this shit was personal. He looked up and saw Foot standing beside his bed.

"Hey lil' soldier you made it, huh? I wish Puff was as tough as you, but he's still in a coma...so what the hell happened? I got here as fast as I could," Foot said.

Bobby took a deep breath then began to talk. His mouth was kind of dry so his voice cracked.

"I'm glad you could make it. I'm sorry you had to see me like this, but I tried. I really did," Bobby said.

"That's life, you can't win them all. Sometimes we have to lose. It's being able to play again that makes us winners," Foot said.

"I don't know how them fools found my house. At first I was thinking that it may have been Monique, but I guess Brigit told them," Bobby said.

"Yea I was thinking the same thing. Her family is not doing so well. They said it's my fault. They think some jackers might have followed me home. They're taking care of her body, her mom is having her cremated this week," Foot said.

"I'm sorry to hear that. How is Monique?" Bobby asked, he attempted to try to sit up, but he was still too weak. Monique was Bobby's girlfriend. She had been at the house when Bobby was shot and had taken a hell of a blow to the head.

"She straight, worried about you, but she's ok. She told me to tell you if you woke up, that she loves you," Foot said.

"Man, them nigga's caught me slipping. I had just got through getting that package ready for Wayne. At first I heard a scream, and then a man's voice. I figured it was that Wayne nigga on some bullshit trying to take something, so I just ran out busting. When I got in the living room I noticed it was two niggas. I thought I had hit one, but he must have been Robo Cop...nigga just stood there. Next thing I know the other nigga lets off one on me and I was down," Bobby said.

"Did you see the nigga's faces?" Foot asked.

"Hell yea, I seen they faces. They wasn't trying to hide. As a matter of fact they left you a message. It was your boy Justus and that Brick nigga. They told me to tell you thanks for the raise," Bobby said frowning.

"I thought that nigga was dead."

"Turns out Darrel snatched the wrong body. That was his momma that was killed. He want blood...he's pissed," said Bobby.

"Do you blame him? It's casualties of war. That nigga was a dead man walking anyway…a nigga don't take nothing from Foot. I'm gonna make these niggas pay the piper. Did they get everything?" Foot asked.

"Yea, they got everything. I don't usually put the money with the work, but I was about to drop the work off and meet you," Bobby said.

Foot began shaking his head, "They'll be releasing you today, and I don't care what it takes you find my money Bobby!" Foot said, then turned and walked out of the room.

....

"Ding Dong," the door bell sounded like an old alarm clock.

Brick's girlfriend Shawn was in the kitchen cooking.

"Who is it?" she yelled turning the eye down on the stove, so that it wouldn't burn her chicken. She headed to the door, "Who is it?" she yelled again.

"It's me girl. Open the door," Brick said.

"Why you ain't using your key?" Shawn said opening the door.

"My hands are full," Brick said stepping through the door carrying two large duffle bags.

Justus was behind him carrying duffle bags, too.

"It smells good in here Shawn, what you cooking? I know you're feeding your boy, I'm starving," Justus said.

"Boy you know you're welcome whenever, so stop that. I'm cooking fried chicken, macaroni, potatoes and that sweet bread that you like," Shawn said.

"Sounds good to me," Justus said.

"Hey baby, how's my sweetheart?" Brick said making his way to the bedroom with Justus following close behind.

"Don't 'hey sweetheart' me nigga. Where in the hell have you been and what the hell you got in those bags?" Shawn said.

"I've been working," Brick said locking the door to the bedroom.

He unzipped the bags and sat the ones with the bricks on the floor sliding them under the bed. Then he poured the bag with the money out onto the bed, and neatly stacked it everywhere: 20s, 50s and 100s. Justus smiled. They began counting the money. An hour or so had passed before they finished...it totaled $223,000.

"Not bad, not bad at all," Justus said.

"Not bad? Nigga we did it big this time. 20 bricks and 223 stacks, son that's never look back money," Brick said holding the cash up and kissing it.

CHAPTER 6

JACKPOT!!!

Two weeks later the twin '76 Cutlass drop tops hogged the streets. Jolly rancher green paint with lambo doors, 28 inch spinning ashanties with white leather interior. Enough wood to make a wood pecker jealous. Justus' bucket seats were custom made; he had 'R.I.P Pam' stitched in all of his head rests. He had spent a fortune at Hollywood Car Customs, but it was all worth it. Every time he got inside he felt his mother's presence with him. Nothing on the streets could touch it. He and Brick tailed each other down Lichey Ave. With their doors up, high rims spinning. Brick stood up with one hand on his wheel, head bobbing like a mad man waiving his Tec in the air. They circled the block a couple of times watching the crowd cheer them on, niggas were jumping up and down, women were screaming and kids gave chase. Brick felt like a star. All his life he had dreamed of this kind of money. No more standing on the corner. The small piece life was over and there wasn't a bitch in the hood that he couldn't have. Shawn even seemed to notice. Lately she had become insecure as ever. No matter how many lavish gifts he showered her with. Tiffany's just wasn't enough.

Bobby was stressed. He didn't know where to begin looking to find Foot's money. He had never been faced with a situation like this. Out of all the birds he had sold in his lifetime, he'd never been jacked. He figured cats couldn't be that stupid, he was known for slanging iron. But it had been a year or so since the last time he'd burned some ass and the respect he once had was wearing off. That's how it was in the hood. You had to constantly prove yourself, other wise you wasn't shit.

It was going on three weeks since he had been released from the hospital and so far his hands had turned up nothing. Foot was losing his patience and he was starting to get worried. What if they no longer had the money? He had kept his ears to the streets. Rumor was that Justus and Brick had copped some mean ass rides like some shit you'll see in a Donk magazine. Darrel was on the lookout, something would break soon. Bobby pulled his Escalade in the parking lot of Dan's Market, looked around, parked and jumped out. He didn't even bother turning on his alarm, if a nigga was that stupid he could die today.

"Hey man you got a couple dollars? I'm stranded and I'm trying to get back home. I'm from New York," the man said standing next to the entrance holding a brown paper bag. Bobby was in no mood for games. He had heard that line a thousand times and if a nigga wanted to con him he'd have to do better than that so he decided to play his own games, "Sho' 'nough...I'm from New York. What part you from B? You don't sound like you from the city son," Bobby put on his fake New York accent.

"Aww I'm from Brooklyn," the man said nodding his head showing off his crooked teeth.

"Me, too. Pitkin Ave. So where you hang?...I've never seen you around." Bobby knew Pitkin Avenue well. Whenever he was in New York he'd visit Masjid Abu Hanifah and pay his respect.

"I'm all over the big apple, you might see me anywhere," the man said lying through his teeth.

"Dig that so? What's your name? I like to at least know the name of the people I talk to," Bobby said holding the door to the store open, one foot inside.

"All I'm sorry B, my name is Mike," the man said,

"Man, that's crazy son. My name is Mike, too...hell naw. I guess we was meant to meet, hey look I'm about to run in this store and grab some cigars and we can buss a few blocks and get to know each other...smoke something you feel me?" Bobby said,

Mike didn't want to blow his cover. Plus, if he played his cards right he could get more than a few dollars. Hell he was already being offered weed.

"Sounds good to me...I'll be waiting right here," the man said.

Bobby went into the store and purchased a Gatorade, a box of cigarillos and a couple of lottery tickets. He waived at the cashier and hurried out of the store. The man followed Bobby back to his Escalade and got in. Bobby put in BG's Chopper City CD and pulled off. They had been riding for about two minutes when the man said, "Hey yo Mike, if you want me to I'll roll up while you drive...where's the weed?"

Bobby smiled and turned onto a side street bringing the Escalade to a complete stop. He reached under his seat then pulled out a 45 ruger and pointed it at the so called 'Mike'.

"I ain't smoking no weed, but I'll smoke yo' ass if you try me. It's niggas like you that gives niggas like me a bad name. Now empty them pockets fool and throw everything on the floor then get the hell out of here before I blow a hole in your lying ass," Bobby said,

"What part of the game is this B?" the man said removing a small roll of money from his pocket and tossing it on the floor along with a pack of Newports.

"Open the door slowly fool and put your hands up," Bobby said.

The man did as he was told. "Come on Mike. Don't do this. We could be partners man, I like you," the man said hands raised to the sky. Bobby picked the wallet up off the floor then pulled out an ID. The picture was that of the man, but his name was Tommy, Tommy Allgood from Tennessee.

"You know you shouldn't keep stuff like this lying around Tommy, somebody might find it...for pulling that lame ass game I should kill you. So how does it feel to be tricked fool? Not so good does it?...Better luck next time, I suggest you find you a new hustle because that Mike from New York shit gone get you put in a box." Bobby pulled off. It was time for him to go back to work, but without any product that would be impossible. He thought about calling Foot, but quickly changed his mind. He had twenty stacks stashed away at his trap house for a rainy day. He dreaded having to start all over, but that was life. It comes easy it goes easy. His whip game was superb. He'd have no problem turning one into two and with his clientele he would be back on his feet in no time, a simple plan.

"Low Don wants to know what's the hold up. You seem to be running behind, which is bad for business...is there a problem?" Cain said into the phone to Foot..

"Not at all. I mean nothing that I can't handle so tell Low I need a few more days and I'm sorry for the inconvenience. I'll make it up to him I promise...some shit came up on my end, plus them folks been hot, but I'm getting it together now," Foot said. This shit with Bobby had put him in between a rock and a hard place. He was never slow with the connect, that was a for sure death sentence. If he had to go in his stash he'd be almost dry and he had come too far to start from scratch. Low would just have to wait, slow money was better than no money. And if they pushed him too hard they wouldn't get shit, but Foot was in no shape to fight a war and Low had an army of niggas on stand by waiting to kill. He knew because he was one of them.

Cain mumbled something under his breath, "Well hurry, the Don is waiting," he said disconnecting the phone.

"So this is what being the man is like. I could get use to this," Brick thought to himself.

Justus had put him in charge of the coke and he was loving the attention that the drugs brought him. Overnight he had went from being Brick the thug to Brick the birdman. Sitting in his drop top at the drive-thru of Checkers, he thumbed through a stack of one hundred dollar bills. The car in front of him pulled off and he pulled up to the window, rims still spinning, music banging, a cute young lady wearing a red hat came to serve him.

"Nice car, baby. That whip killing anyone I've seen, it looks like the paint still wet...what color is it? Can I touch it?" the lady said. Brick seized the opportunity to floss. He raised the driver side door up and placed the wad of cash on his lap smiling.

"Get in, you can do more than touch it...what's your name, baby girl?" Brick asked,

"My name is Resha. What's yours?" she asked.

"The streets call me Brick, but you can call me Money Bag or Superman, so let a nigga save you," Brick said.

"Boy you know that you got a woman, so don't play with me Superman. I'm not the one, I'm crazy," Resha said tossing her head back as she laughed.

"I'm crazy too, baby. We can go crazy together. So what's your number?" Brick asked.

A tan 2012 Ford Taurus pulled up behind Brick and began to blow. Brick ignored the driver, he was on a mission.

"What makes you think that I want you to call me?" Resha said smiling. "And what do you want to eat? Have you forgot you haven't ordered?"

"I ain't even hungry really, but what's up thoe? You don't want me calling? I feel you, your loss," Brick said and let his door down.

"Boy, I was just playing. I know you ain't getting mad," Resha said.

"I don't get mad baby, I get money. But what makes you think that I wanted to play?" Brick said.

"578-6932 nigga don't come calling me sometime next week or I'm not gonna know your ass. As a matter of fact, what's your number?" Resha said. They exchanged numbers and Brick rode off into the sun feeling like the star he was. He thought about how his life had changed, he even thought about his enemies. If push came to shove he'd kill, no doubt about it, he was ready. Since the drama had started he had already copped some heavy artillery; two AR15's, two Glock 40's and a mini 14. Fatso had even tried to get him to buy some C4, he declined. He told him that if he needed it he'd let him know, but what he did need was a connect. He was running out of coke and he didn't know where to begin to shop. Fatso had told him that he was checking into it. He knew some cats on the south side that kept that work and it wouldn't be a problem getting him hooked up, it was just a matter of time. He had been sightseeing for about an hour when his cell phone began to ring.

"What's up nigga? Where you at?" Justus said.

"What's up fool? I'm out here on the north side, but I'm headed east now. What's good?" Brick said.

"Aww just checking on you bruh, I didn't want nothing…Oh, I did run into Pete about an hour ago. Said that he had something he was trying to give you," Justus said.

"Yea, he need to have something to give me because I've been looking for that fool. I gave him a lil' half time and he been dodging me. I had a bullet with his name on it about them stacks," Brick said and adjusted his rearview mirror. Either he was high or the same gray truck that he had seen parked at

Checkers was now behind him. He sped up to see if the truck would speed up too. It appeared to be trying to catch up with his Cutlass. He removed one of his twin Glock 40s from under his seat.

"Hey bruh, anybody you know drive a gray dodge truck?" Brick asked.

"Naw, not that I know of. Why you ask?" Justus asked puzzled.

"I may be tripping, but it looks like the same truck has been behind me for the past hour."

"Have you been smoking nigga?" Justus asked.

"Naw, bruh. No purple haze, I'm sober as a judge. Hold on for a second," Brick said making a sudden right turn onto a side street. The gray truck kept straight. He was trying to see who was in it, but the windows were tinted and all he could see was a head.

"Looks like I may be tripping. I turned off and they kept straight," Brick said removing his finger from the trigger, he relaxed.

"I told you nigga you spooked," Justus laughed. "It's ok to be spooked it keeps a nigga on his toes and being on your toes keeps you alive," Justus said.

Upside Down

CHAPTER 7

HARD WORK NO PLAY!!!

Resha was exhausted, Checkers just didn't pay enough for all the hard work she did. She figured she should at least be manager by now. Her body ached from all the twisting, turning and bending, and to top it off her clothes reeked of onions. She ran her bath water and decided to soak, she could use it. She couldn't get Brick off of her mind, which was strange because after her last relationship she really wasn't interested in men at all. They seemed to be all the same, full of shit. She picked up the cordless phone and dialed his number, he answered on the first ring.

"Yea."

"Superman I'm drowning," she said sinking into the bubble filled tub, the water felt good to her skin. She was a soap freak and had over thirty bottles of soft soap body wash, everything from coconut to peach pie.

"Call batman baby, I'm busy. There's a cat stuck in a tree," Brick said.

"Nigga you full of it. I ain't got time for this...bye." Resha had gotten pissed off and was about to hang up.

"Hold on, wait a second baby. I'm just playing, calm down," Brick said.

"What makes you think that I want to play?" Resha was being sarcastic reminding him of what he had said when they first met. "Aww you got game girl. I like you," Brick said turning his radio down, the custom 18inch subwoofers made it hard to hear.

"What you doing?" Resha said.

"Nothing really...out here on my paper route getting what's mine, plus trying to dodge these cases you know what I mean? Where you at sexy?" Brick said.

"I'm at home. I just got off from work, tired as hell, sitting here in the bathtub," she took her hand and smacked the water making a splash. Brick instantly became aroused. He pictured her naked body wet with suds running down the crack of her juicy ass.

"I see, ain't nothing wrong with that... so where is home? Hope that I'm not being nosey. I promise I won't stalk you, it ain't in me," Brick said.

"Nigga, please. You'd do more than stalk me. I'll have to get a restraining order to keep your ass away because I'm a real woman nigga. I'll have you busting out windows and flattening tires talking 'bout you sprung," Resha said.

"Damn just disrespect a boss. It's that serious? You're scaring me," Brick said,

"You better be scared... Do you know where Red Shield center is?" Resha asked.

"Yea," Brick said.

"I live behind Red Shield on Berry Street, in the big yellow house. It's the only one on the street, you can't miss it."

"What are you saying?" Brick asked,

"Are you deaf boy? Just swing by," Resha said.

Resha's house was laid to the bone, wall to wall carpet, fish tanks and expensive art covered her walls. The living room was black and gold all the way down to the glass tables. You could tell that whoever had picked the furniture had nice taste.

"I must say that I'm impressed. So who you got living up in here, Scarface?" Brick said reclining on the soft leather. He took his shoes off so that he could feel the soft carpet under his feet. For some reason he always did that. He liked the way it tickled his toes. He glanced around the house admiring the scenery. There was some writing on a picture that appeared to be Arabic. He squinted his eyes and tried to make out the letters.

"This is really a nice place," he thought. The thought of some crazy ass boyfriend busting in the door, asking all kinds of questions that he didn't care to answer, made him uneasy. He rubbed his 40 glock and took a deep breath.

"May I get you something to drink?" Resha asked,

"Yea Moet would be fine," he said jokingly.

"Boy I ain't got no Moet. How 'bout some tea or water?" Resha asked.

"Tea is good. I'm really not a big water fan. When I was little I almost drowned and ever since then me and water ain't been all that cool," Brick said.

"Boy you're silly. I take it you can't swim too good either, huh?" she said.

"Well, it depends…in water…. no," Brick said smiling showing twenty gold teeth. Resha picked up the remote control and turned the TV on.

"So what do you want to watch? I got cable and DVDs, just name it," she said.

Brick smiled. The look in his eyes said it all. "I'd rather watch you baby. I'm not really all that big on TV, too much going on in the real world to be trapped in a box." He watched the way her ass moved as she walked into the kitchen. The things he wanted to do to her.

"So who stays here with you?" he finally asked,

"Nobody I stay by myself; no kids, no man, nobody," Resha replied.

"I find that hard to believe. I mean a woman as fine as you all alone in this big ass house. Where's your man at?" Brick asked, at that moment he realized he had made a mistake. Her mood seemed to darken and her face told a story. She hesitated for a minute, it had been so long since she had been asked that question. She wished he had never even asked, the memories were too painful. She could remember it like yesterday.

"Well let's see," she said taking a deep breath. Then she began. "About three years ago my ole man was killed in a car accident; a drunken Mexican hit him head on. He died instantly," she said with tears welling up in her eyes. He could see she was about to cry and changed the subject.

"Sorry to hear that...what's up with all those pots in there? You don't be cooking, all that china for decoration," he said patting his belly.

"Yea right. I be getting down boy don't let my job fool you, I ain't no slouch. I don't live off fast food, momma taught me well. I've only been with one man in my life and we was married so I hope you didn't get the wrong idea about me. I just called you because I wanted some company, nothing else I can assure you," Resha said. Brick felt like a fool. He had never been turned down so nicely. He wanted to cry, but the funny thing about it was that he wasn't mad. Sure he would love to fuck her brains out, who wouldn't? She had it going on, but he understood and more than anything he respected her mind and her strength. He had never met anyone like her before. She was unique in every way.

"Resha you're special baby and I'm not just saying this. I wish that every woman I've met was like you, no doubt. I like you and I would be lying to say that I didn't want to tap that, but I understand you." Suddenly his phone vibrated and he had received a text. "Excuse me," he said looking at his phone. The message read, "Good news Fatso is waiting. Meet me at the spot...one love, Justus." Indeed that was good news. Fatso had found the work, it was time to re-up.

"Hey baby look something just came up. I'm sorry, but I have to rush. I really would like to see you again maybe we could grab some dinner." Brick put on his shoes and headed for the door, she followed.

"You know Brick it's something about you. I don't know what it is yet, but I'll figure it out." She walked him outside. They were standing on the porch when a white Camaro pulled up, parked and out jumped two men, Brick reached for his glock 40. Resha saw the look on his face and she knew it meant trouble, she had forgotten to mention that she had a baby brother that came by to check on her often.

"Brick this my lil' brother, Wayne, and his friend. You're cool he's only sixteen and swear he's a thug." She introduced them to one another, "Wayne this is my friend Brick," Resha said. Wayne hated when she did that even though he was younger than his sister by about ten years. He hated when she called him 'little brother' especially in front of other people. It made him feel small and he was definitely no punk.

"What's up lil man?" Brick said.

"The name is Wayne son, ain't nothing about me little...what you doing with my sister?" Wayne said with his chest stuck out and his best mean mug on. He was trying his hardest to look tough. Brick was shocked, he couldn't believe this lil nigga was trying to challenge him, he smiled.

"Me and your sister cool. You better get used to seeing me around."

Resha interrupted, "Wayne shut up, I'm grown I can take care of myself." She knew that Wayne was very protective when it came to her, he had been like that all of his life.

"No, no it's ok. I understand the lil nigga.

He's just doing what he should. I don't blame him," Brick said extending his arm in an attempt to shake Wayne's hand. Brick was so busy talking that he didn't notice the gray truck across the street watching him until it pulled off.

CHAPTER 8

MOVING ON UP!!!

"It's a three bedroom, two baths, there's a walk-in closet over there to the left, plenty of space, nice shelves, shoe rack, you can almost live in there," the landlord said jokingly as he gave Justus a tour of his new apartment.

Justus was in love at first sight. Since his mom had been killed he hadn't been staying at home, too many bad memories. He needed the new apartment just as bad as he needed air. Plus he had to get low just in case the killers decided to swing back by. This condo was in Daisy Forest, home to some of the wealthiest people in Nashville. In a way he felt out of place after living in the hood all his life. This place had a tennis court, gym, swimming pool and grass as green as a forest, something else his old neighborhood didn't have.

"I'll take it!" Justus said excited. It was everything he'd ever dreamed of. He just wished his mother was around to see it.

"I figured that you would. Sign here and there's a $2,000 deposit and $1,100 rent per month...oh, no pets," the landlord said.

"I have a cat, but I wouldn't call it a pet. He's more like a person, would that be a problem?" Justus asked.

"Well a cat wouldn't hurt I guess, but be sure to keep it inside, no roaming," the landlord said.

"No problem he's a house cat anyway," Justus replied.

"Good. Here's your key," the landlord said.

"Yea who's the man? You owe me big time for this one nigga," Darrel said excitedly into the phone.

"What the hell you talking 'bout fool and make this quick I'm in the kitchen," Bobby said standing over the stove, Pyrex in one hand, clothes hanger in the other sweating like a fein. Junky Tommy was standing look out at the door with a pump shotgun. He had been given orders to shoot first and ask questions later. So anything without a badge was getting shot, but he wasn't about to kill no cops, everybody knew that you don't kill cops.

"Guess who lives on Berry Street?" Darrel said.

"Who fool?...I don't have time for charades. I'm Betty Crocker right now and you want to play," Bobby said leaning the Pyrex to one side. He added more baking soda and watched the dope rock up before his eyes.

"Not at all bruh. Get this, I seen it with my own eyes...Brick! And the nigga was with his girlfriend standing in the yard. I had been following him earlier, but lost him when he turned off. I think he had a feeling that somebody was trailing him and at that time I wasn't a hundred percent if it was him or not. I was just trying to get them damn spinners, the nigga got to be sitting on some damn twenty eights or something in a drop that looks like a big foot in the street. I ain't lying son, it was him no doubt. I looked him dead in his face when I rode by the house," Darrel said imagining all the sick twisted things he would do when he caught Justus. Perhaps he would dismember his body and eat his heart, yea that would be nice. Or maybe he would tie him up and rape him repeatedly while Brick watched and waited his turn. The thought made his dick hard.

"Let me get this straight, you just saw the nigga that robbed me?" Bobby asked.

"Hell yea," Darrel said happily.

"And you didn't kill him? Nigga what the hell is wrong with you?...you had my money under your nose and you let it slip away!" Bobby was in a rage, he was yelling at the top of his lungs and his eyes had turned bloodshot red. He turned and slung the glass jar into the wall sending glass and dope flying everywhere. Tommy stood there looking, he desperately wanted to try and save the dope, but he didn't think that would be a good idea right now. He had never seen Bobby so angry.

"Bruh, I know where he lives, you're not hearing me. I know where he lives and I didn't shoot because Justus wasn't with him. I wanted to kill two birds with one stone. What's the sense in getting one and letting the other one get away? What if Justus is the one with the money? We hit Brick and he goes into hiding. You know how long it took us to find these niggas," Darrel said.

Bobby was listening. Darrel had his full attention, what he was saying made sense. He didn't want to make a mistake like that then the money would be lost forever. He was starting to calm down. All the shit he had been through in the last month was starting to wear him down. He took a seat at the kitchen table and stared at the floor. His mind was racing a hundred miles an hour. He picked up his 45 off the table and squeezed it tightly, it felt so good in his palm. He pictured himself aiming it at Justus' head and pulling the trigger over and over and over again until he was unrecognizable.

"Ok I see what you're saying. It makes sense now," Bobby said.

"Yea bruh," Darrel said.

"Don't let me down and if you think that you can't handle it let me know. And I'm on my way this is important to me. I want bloodshed," Bobby said.

Fatso was sitting in his black 2011 Silverado pickup truck in the park when Justus and Brick arrived. Justus was driving. They pulled in beside Fatso and killed the engine. It was a beautiful day, kids ran to and from playing freeze tag, swinging and sliding, the smell of fresh flowers was in the air and the breeze was just enough to put you to sleep.

"What it do Fats?" Justus said exiting the car.

"You got it baby, one day at a time, slow motion. Look I got some good news and some bad news, so what you want first?" Fatso said.

"Give us the good you keep the bad," Brick said.

"Well, first of all, did you bring the paper?" Fatso asked.

"Of course we got it. It's in the car now, $200 stacks," Justus said.

"Good, the bad news is that the connect doesn't want to meet you. Right now he wants to make sure that your money is good. You know, get to know you. I told him that you were my people and I put my word on that, he trust me so he sent the work with me," Fatso said.

"Damn that's real. You mean you got it right now?"

"You damn straight I got it right now," Fatso said.

"So what's the bad news?" Brick said confused.

"I'm not leaving this park with it. You'll have to mule your own dope. I've been 'bout to have a baby with all of this snow in my truck," Fatso said, they all laughed.

"Yo Fats we really appreciate this," Justus said reaching into the car and grabbing the duffle bag full of money. They made the exchange.

"He told me to tell you if you're not a hundred percent satisfied he'd return your dough straight fish scale. You want to bust a couple of them open and see...go ahead," Fatso asked.

"No need baby we trust you," Justus said giving Fatso dap.

"Good so when you gone let me drive that car?...I want to ride fly too nigga," Fatso threw his hands up in the air like a bird.

"Anytime bruh, anytime," Justus said.

Justus sat at Brick's kitchen table counting the bricks, Shawn was nowhere to be found. On the table was a note Brick didn't even bother to read it.

"20 bricks...you know I was thinking bruh, maybe we should have copped 50. Ain't no sense in holding back. We started off with 20 of them thangs, niggas that's really getting money spend it all. The more coke we got the more money we make," Brick said.

"I bet if we bought 50 he'd dump a hundred on us with no problem." He was standing in the middle of the floor giving his Nino Brown speech.

"You know the money has been good. I ain't gone lie, but I ain't really trying to make a career out of this shit. Let's not fool ourselves, every nigga that plays this game loses and there's no way to win. Remember Lil Mechi? He was heavy in the game, the police couldn't catch him so they killed him...Low Hard Baller's click, you remember them niggas? Low got life in the Feds, Paul Woods, Big Russell, Rabbit.... you name it, same ending," Justus said shaking his head.

"Yea, but those niggas was greedy. Man look at Paul, he had more money than Master P. Fool made ova 300 million a year and wouldn't stop, that's just stupid," Brick said.

"Everybody says that when they're on the outside looking in it's easier said than done. That kind of money sucks you in like crack and you become sprung, niggas can't just walk out alive. How you think Sosa gone feel when you tell him you're trying to change your life, but you've been all up in his house just last week with his family?...naw you know too much, you got to die," Justus said.

"Yea, but I still say that we should have a goal, something easy to reach like a few million. Once we get it we stop," Brick said.

"You just don't get it do you?" Justus said.

CHAPTER 9

"HOT BOY"

Lil Sam was fresh out the joint, a real live hot boy. He was already on three bonds and had just got caught with a half of a kilo the week prior. Somehow he had gotten out of jail again. He was working with them folks. He sat in the parking lot of Subway waiting on Brick to pull up. He was supposed to be purchasing a kilo of powder, but the circumstances had him a little nervous. He had never worn a wire before, This would be the first time. He hoped Brick was alone just in case something went wrong, he figured he could handle Brick, but Justus was a motherfucker. Chances were he'd be strapped.

Brick pulled into the parking lot and parked next to Sam's Yukon XL, he was driving an all black Altima. Sam waved for Brick to get out and come to the truck, but Brick just sat there. Finally Sam got the message and got out the truck and walked over to the car.

"Damn you blind or something nigga? I know you seen me waving. You got me walking with all this money on me and the police hotter than the Fourth of July out here," he said getting into the car.

"But you wanted me to get out the car and stroll across the lot like Santa Clause with a bag of dope?...I don't know why you had me to meet you at this hot ass Subway anyway. Ain't this where the Feds busted Big Wayne?" Brick said surveying the parking lot.

"I don't know nothing about the Feds nigga we could have met somewhere else if you had said something," Sam said looking around.

"Didn't you just catch a case not too long ago?" Brick asked.

"Who me?...Hell naw. Don't wish that on me, I'm already on one or two bonds now. I can't afford another case, another case would kill me. Where's the dope?" Sam asked.

"Where is the money at nigga? I got the work, we're going to count this paper first," Brick said.

"The paper already counted nigga, my money good. You don't ever got to count mines. If anything I'm going to be over, but never short," Sam said reaching in his pants and pulling out a small brown sack full of money.

"Here it is right here. What are you charging me for this key?" Sam asked.

"Same thing I told you over the phone," Brick said.

"I can't remember what you told me, what was it?" Sam asked again.

"Fool you mean you got a bag of money that ain't short, but you don't even know what the hell I charged you?"

Sam wasn't making any sense. "I still haven't saw the dope yet. Here's the money, where's the dope?" Sam said holding the money into the air like a flag waiving it back and forth. Brick was starting to get pissed off. Something was wrong, he could feel it. And all of a sudden the parking lot had become full of strange looking cars and too many people reading newspapers. He thought fast following his first instinct.

"Aww Sammy is that what you said 'dope'? I thought you said 'soap'...I don't mess with no drugs man. I've been selling Avon for months trying to make an honest buck, you got the wrong man."

"What the hell is wrong with you? You know damn well that I don't want no soap I want dope...look man if you don't trust me I can take my business somewhere else!" Sam said angrily.

"If you want some dope that's what you gone have to do because I sell soap...Avon soap, black soap, shea butter soap, that's it," Brick said.

Sam felt like a dummy, this mistake could have cost him his life. Embarrassed he got out of the car and headed back to his truck. Brick pulled off behind him, he blew the horn to get Sam's attention. Sam stopped turning his head around. Brick stopped beside him and rolled the window down.

"Hey Sam tell them if they want me they have to do better than that, you look like a snitch!" he said laughing as he pulled off.

....

"Bruh, I'm telling you the nigga was wired. I could see it in his face. Fool kept saying 'where's the dope, where's the dope' then all of a sudden all these cars appeared out of nowhere, people jogging, reading news papers. Come on man it was so easy to see, I should have killed that nigga...I can't believe I let him walk away!" Brick said pacing the living room floor of Justus' condo.

"Naw you did right. If the nigga was wired then the cops was probably all over the place," Justus said.

"Ain't no if to it bruh. I'm telling you the nigga didn't even know how much money he had," Brick said.

See this is what I was warning you about, nigga it's wicked out here ain't no love. So what you lucked up and peeped it this time, but what happens when you don't?...you go down, down in history as a nigga that once had money, but in the end ain't got shit," Justus said shaking his head. He got up from the couch, walked over to the window and peeped out.

"What do you see when you look outside Brick?" Justus asked.

"Cars, vans, the sky, a few birds," Brick responded.

"That's right nigga... freedom. Who in the hell wants to be a bird without wings?" Justus said.

Foot and Bobby were eating lunch at McDonalds on the out skirts of town. Foot felt comfortable meeting there since it was hardly ever any traffic, just nice old white folk. He doubted that anybody would ever recognize him here. He bit into his McChicken then chased it with a couple of fries.

"Man these fries stale as hell, they must have cooked these last night," Foot said squirting more ketchup onto his fries.

"They ain't never fresh here, I'm starting to think that's how white folk like their fries," Bobby laughed.

"And I'm starting to think you just done took my money!" Foot said,

Bobby suddenly stopped laughing and looked Foot dead in his eyes.

"Man bruh, you know I'll never take nothing from you…you tripping. I'm loyal and you know it, if there's anybody you can trust you know it's me…we been through hell together nigga. You're like my brother I never had and if I could have stopped them niggas from taking the money, I would have and you know this," Bobby said.

Foot and Bobby had grown up together. He could tell when Bobby was lying or telling the truth.

"I believe you, it's just that Low Don don't want to hear no 'can I pay you later' or 'some niggas done robbed me' shit. Man, this kind of money can get you and me killed...I ain't never been late with the paper, now all of a sudden I'm down. I got like a hundred G's to my name and some niggas on the loose with my bricks and the connect wants his money. I'm about to pull that mask out," Foot said.

"Bruh, relax. I'm telling you I got this under control. Just let your hair down and get you some fresh air. You've been thinking too much and I know you miss Brigit, but the sun is still shining. Why don't you go out and have some fun. Look, there's a new sports bar on 2nd Avenue. I hear it's nice, good food and pretty ladies. Why don't you check it out and leave the hard work to me?"

"That don't sound like a bad idea, you know you might be right," Foot said massaging his temples. He took a swallow of his coke and tossed the empty cup into a nearby trash can.

"I know I'm right. Try it you'll see," Bobby said.

2nd Avenue was jumping, anybody who was anybody seemed to be there. Ted's Sports and Grill was packed with athletes, doctors and all kind of business people, you name it. Foot sat at the bar eyeing the plasma screen on the wall. TVs were everywhere, he began to count them then he thought to himself. Maybe Bobby was right, maybe he did need to get out more.

Since Brigit had been murdered he'd been isolated. Too much seemed to be going on and he had to stay focused. Sure money wasn't everything, but it sure made life much easier. He reflected over the past months events, what the hell was going on anyway? What had started all of this confusion? Things were running so smoothly until somebody tried to kill him. It was his order that had gotten Fat Tony killed. Surely Tony's home boys, 'The Outlaws' wanted revenge. The question was when. It was his order that made Justus a marked man. He felt responsible for his mother's killing… in a way he was. He didn't blame Justus for wanting to kill him. If the shoe was on the other foot, somebody would have hell to pay. He was starting to stress himself out just thinking about it. He had too much on his mind, he needed a drink. He called for the bartender.

"Excuse me," Foot said.

"Yes how may I help you?" A man wearing a t-shirt saying 'I'm drunk and I'm proud' came to his aid.

"Long island iced tea and thank you," Foot said.

"Long island iced tea…a little soft ain't it buddy? You look like a Bombay or Patron man," the bartender said.

"Not even close...I don't even really drink, just trying to get a buzz," Foot said.

"Oh really? Well you'll get a buzz for sure, no doubt about that because I make the best long island iced tea in Nashville," he said while mixing and shaking a bottle. Foot sat and watched. He couldn't help to notice the pretty young lady that had just sat down next to him. She was wearing an all black Fendi dress and black high heels. Foot had always been kind of shy around women, he wanted to speak but didn't know what to say.

Suddenly she spoke, "Are you going to buy a lady a drink or what?" she said smiling.

"Why not, what do you drink?" Foot asked.

She had beautiful eyes and some of the prettiest teeth he'd ever seen, her skin was flawless. As a matter of fact, she was drop dead gorgeous.

"It depends, tonight I'm drinking what you're drinking," she said.

"Cool, sounds good to me," Foot said and called for the bartender to bring another long island iced tea.

"So what brings you out? I don't think I've ever seen you around here before," she said.

Foot turned around to face her. Something about the woman made him feel comfortable, he wanted to talk, wanted to open up to someone. Maybe that would make him feel better, he had a lot on his chest that needed getting off and she seemed like she was a good listener.

"Well where do I begin? For starts this month has been hell, I've lost almost everything that I owned: my money, my woman, my friend, even almost lost my life and right now I don't know if I'm coming or going," Foot said shaking his head. He took a long swallow of long island iced tea and placed the glass back on the counter. Puff was his nigga. No matter what they went through he always had his back and now because of him Puff was almost dead.

"Oh I wish there was something that I could do to help you, you seem so nice," she said offering a friendly smile.

"I wish there was something I could do to help myself," Foot said. He tossed his head back and gazed at the ceiling as if at any moment the answer to his problems would fall from the sky.

"You got to keep the faith and things will get better," she said in an attempt to comfort Foot.

"When?" Foot said with a strange look on his face.

"See there it's getting better already. I just seen a smile, that's a start. You know one thing I try to always remember when I'm feeling down is that there's someone else feeling worse than me," the lady said.

"That's true," Foot said.

It had been a long time since he had met someone as positive as this woman. She seemed to have had an answer for everything. He could tell she was a strong black woman, the kind that has no business in a bar.

"We all have things that we go through. That's life," she said sipping her drink.

"Yea so what brings you out? And don't tell me that you just didn't have anything better to do than come to a bar and drink because I'm not buying that," Foot said turning his body sideways so that they were face to face. He looked deep into her eyes, she reminded him of someone.

"Honestly I had a few things on my mind also, nothing really worth talking about," she said. Her legs were long, Foot wondered how tall she must really be. He loved amazons.

"Come on don't give me that. If it's on your mind then it's worth talking about and I want to listen....hell it's the least I can do," Foot said sounding sincere.

"Have you ever felt used by someone that you really care about, but it's so bad that you're not even sure if they care about you?" she asked. Her eyes had become glossy.

"The love thing, huh?" Foot asked.

"I don't know what to call it, but I was told that love ain't supposed to hurt and this is killing me. Maybe it's hate, doesn't love suppose to feel good?" she asked.

"I guess. I mean I guess that you would have to be in love to know and right now I'm just in stress," Foot said laughing.

"But have you ever been in love?" she asked.

"That's a good question. All I know is I want to be in love, but every time I think I've found someone that really cares about me and the things that I hold dear, it turns out that they hate me. And I'm starting to think that love is a bunch of crap and if it's not then why is it such a pain in the ass?" Foot said looking around the bar, it was starting to thin out. Time had flown by. People were saying their goodbyes and heading home.

"So what's your name, if you don't mind me asking? I loved talking to you and don't get me wrong, but who are you?" Foot said smiling. They had gotten so engaged in conversation they hadn't bothered to exchange names.

"I thought you'd never ask. My name is Shawn Conway. What's yours?" Shawn said.

"Oh, my name is Foot," he said.

"Foot? What a name. So why do people call you 'Foot'?" Shawn asked.

Foot had been asked that question all his life, he was used to it. The tag had actually come from his days as a stick up kid. Once in a home invasion he had attempted to kick a door in and broke his foot. When the cops arrived he was passed out on the porch of the house that he was supposed to be robbing. He left on a stretcher and ever since then his friends called him 'Foot'.

"Long story. Maybe one day I'll share it with you, but for now it looks like this place is closing," Foot said standing. He placed a fifty dollar bill on the counter for the bartender.

"Did you come here by yourself?" He asked.

"Yea, sorta kinda," Shawn said.

"Where's your car parked? I'll walk you to your car and we can swap numbers. Maybe we can talk sometimes," Foot said.

"I rode here in a cab actually," Shawn said.

"Well that's just great. I'll take you home..."

"I don't want you going out of your way for me. I'm ok, the cab is fine," Shawn said.

"No it's not! I'm not going out of my way, really. It would be an honor, don't act like that. We'll stop at the store, gas up and I'll have you home in no time."

CHAPTER 10

Foot's tan 750 on twenty two inch blades pulled up to Jerry's Bi-rites. He surveyed the parking lot. He really didn't like getting gas from the neighborhood stores, they kept the gas watered down and bad gas meant bad performance and a 750 was no hooptie. Most hustlers could only dream of owning one. Shawn was impressed. She had never rode in a BMW, hell she hardly ever went out. Brick was always so busy that he barely even noticed her and that was one of the reasons she decided to go to the bar in the first place. It would be her way of getting back at Brick. Maybe he'd pay her some attention, she thought.

"You want something out of here? They got some Cajun hot wings you got to try," Foot said.

"No thank you. I'm still buzzing from the long island, but maybe next time."

"Next time sounds good," Foot said getting out of the car. "Be right back." He walked up to the cashier's window. The clerk sat behind a bullet proof glass because at this time of the night the doors were locked. Too much crazy shit happening and lately clerks who were just trying to make an honest living were being murdered for chump change.

"Thirty on pump one," Foot said sliding the money under a flap then heading back to the car. A man in a black hoodie sweater carrying a small duffle bag appeared from nowhere standing by the gas pumps. He looked hungry.

"Can I pump your gas mister?" the man asked.

Foot knew the man wanted money and he didn't mind helping people out. What goes around comes around, you just never knew when the tables might turn.

"Yea go ahead." Foot got in the car and eye balled Shawn, she was beautiful. He couldn't help himself.

"Do you know him?" Shawn asked nodding her head toward the window?

"Not at all, just a bum trying to make a dollar and I ain't mad at him. Everyday I'm hustling," Foot said smiling as Rick Ross played in the back ground on his CD player. He turned the radio down, the man had finished pumping the gas and was knocking on the driver side window. He rolled the window down and handed the man a five dollar bill.

"Appreciate that bruh," Foot said.

"No problem...Hey you want to buy some CDs man? I got that new 50 Cent and Young Buck," the man said.

"I already have that 50 Cent and I'm not really a Buck fan, he don't like me, but what else you got?" Foot said. The man unzipped his duffle bag and fumbled inside.

"I got tha same thang that I had last time!" the man said removing an all black mini Uzi from the bag. Foot panicked and hit the gas. The car seemed to take flight, rubber burning and white smoke everywhere.

"Get down!" Foot yelled as the BMW climbed the sidewalk. The man took aim at his fleeing target, the Uzi spitting rounds, bullets showered the 750. A bullet slammed into the back window causing the glass to break. Shawn screamed at the top of her lungs while Foot held her head down on his lap and sped out into the street.

"Stay down we're safe now, but I want to make sure we're not being followed," Foot said. Looking into his rearview mirror he switched lanes and turned onto the main street. Shawn was crying, she had never been so scared in her life. She could hardly function and she was having trouble breathing. What had she gotten herself into? If only she had of stayed at home none of this would have happened. She had a million thoughts running through her mind, who was that man in the hoodie? Foot owed her some answers.

"What the hell just happened back there?" she said sobbing and trying to pull herself together.

Foot's mind was racing and he was trying to place the face of the man and what he had said, 'The same thing that I had last time.' Did he know him from somewhere? It was a possibility and he wasn't ruling out anyone. Where did the man come from in the first place? Had he been at the bar? Maybe it was a hit, he thought.

"It's a long story. First let me say that I'm sorry for putting you in danger, it was never my intention. I told you that I was a troubled man when I met you. I promise whoever did this will pay in ways you couldn't imagine," Foot said slamming his fist against the steering wheel.

Shawn was starting to calm down and she was confused.

"So do you know who did this?" Shawn asked.

"Not exactly, but I have an idea. It just don't make sense," Foot said.

Twenty minutes later Foot and Shawn pulled up in the front of Shawn's apartment and Foot apologized again.

"I'm really sorry. I want to see you again, but if you say no I'll understand and I couldn't even be mad at you," Foot said meaning every word he spoke. He had fucked up tonight, first impressions were everything, but he couldn't help that he was a gangster. That's just the way it was. If she planned on getting to know him she better get used to it. Ain't no telling when shit was going to pop off, it was part of his life style. The price you pay for being ghetto rich.

"Look things happen, I'm just glad to be in one piece, but I've never been in a shootout before," Shawn said laughing. Actually all the excitement was turning her on. She could feel herself becoming wet. She grabbed her purse and opened the door slowly.

"I have your number. I'll call you," Shawn said. "And thanks for the ride."

"If you don't call I'll be back over here knocking on your door," Foot said jokingly.

"Boy I'm going to call you, I promise. Now go home and get some rest, it's been a long night and I know you're tired." They said their goodbyes and he watched her walk to the door. Shawn's ass was so fat that it didn't make sense. From the outside the apartment looked nice, what caught his eye is what sat in the driveway. A '76 Cutlass, jolly rancher green on 28 inch rims looking like any moment it could transform into a space ship and fly away. You could tell that whoever it belonged to had bread. You just didn't see shit like that every day, nice he thought.

"Where in the hell have you been? It's three in the morning." Brick said standing in the middle of the living room floor. He had been up all night waiting on Shawn to get home, it was unlike her to just disappear. Something was definitely going on. He was pissed off and his anger was getting the best of him.

Shawn turned around startled, she didn't even see him standing there. She was too busy trying to slip in and quietly lock the door.

"Ah hey baby I didn't realize I was so late. It's been a long night. Me and Kim was playing cards and time kind of slipped away from me. The cab took forever to come," Shawn said placing her purse on the couch. She removed her shoes, her feet were killing her. High heels always seemed to do that, that's one reason why she never liked wearing them.

"Oh so why didn't you call me?" Brick said impatiently.

"I figured you was busy, you know working and all I didn't want to bother you," Shawn said.

As soon as the words left her mouth she knew she had made a mistake. Like a bolt of lightning, Brick shot across the room slamming Shawn into the wall. Wrapping her hair around his hand he punched her in the face. It was the first time he had ever hit Shawn. She was devastated. No man had ever put his hands on her.

"You think I'm stupid don't you slut? Who the hell do I look like?" he said screaming, pulling her hair and ramming her head into the wall.

"Where in the hell have you been?" Brick said foaming like a mad dog. "Is this what you wanted?" he yelled.

"Stop baby you're hurting me. I'm sorry, I went to the bar that's all." Shawn was crying like a baby.

Brick released her hair. She sat up against the wall with her hands on her head.

"I went to a bar on 2nd Avenue. I had a few drinks. It was late so a guy at the bar offered to bring me home. It was closing time and I didn't want to stand outside so I said yes."

"You're a bigger fool than I thought you was. You mean to tell me that you met some nigga at a bar you don't know him from Adam, who could have been a serial killer and you get in his car and brings him where I lay my head? Are you fucking stupid? I can just kill you." Brick said.

"Baby he was no serial killer. I spoke with him and he had enough problems of his own," Shawn said.

"What is his name since you know so damn much and I ain't talking about no nick name," Brick said looking her straight into her eyes he had her right where he wanted her. He knew she didn't know his real name, what kind of nigga goes to a bar and gives out his real name?

"He didn't tell me his real name baby, but if I would have asked him he would have I bet...he called himself Foot," Shawn said. It was as if someone had set fire to Brick's head. He felt like he was melting, like he was fading away. This couldn't be happening not to him. Out of all the niggas she could have met, she had met Foot. He headed for the bedroom immediately and began packing his things.

"Baby what's wrong?" Shawn yelled. "And where are you going...what did I do? Don't leave me like this. I love you," she wailed.

Brick was in no mood for the small talk. He had to move fast. His life depended on it; **She was sleeping with the enemy!!!**

....

"What do you mean you 'missed him'? failure is not acceptable. I send you niggas to do a job and you can't even kill a damn kid. What the hell am I paying you for? Twice he's gotten away. I don't understand this, Dre. Look, if you can't handle it just let me know because maybe you've lost your touch!" Cain yelled into the cell phone pacing back and forth.

"Flight 18 now boarding," the intercom announced. Cain picked up his luggage and headed for security.

"Hey look, Dre. I'm leaving Miami now. I'll be calling you when I land and you better have something good to tell me," Cain said.

"That's what I'm talking about, baby. I don't think I've ate this good since I went to the feast with my man Ali...I'm so full I'm about to pop." Brick was laid back rubbing his stomach smiling. It had been a long time since he had ate at a table like a family.

Resha had invited him over to dinner. He and Wayne were getting to know each other. Wayne really didn't care too much for Brick and he knew it. The lil nigga seemed to have a chip on his shoulder, but Brick tried to be nice anyway.

"What you think about that chicken, Wayne? She put her foot in it didn't she, KFC ain't got nothing on Resha." He laughed making small talk. Wayne didn't seem to find anything funny. He just sat there eating mac and cheese looking out the window.

"So where did you meet my sister at bruh? I mean I know that she's grown and all, but I was just wondering," Wayne asked staring at Brick as if it was the first time he ever seen him. Resha turned around from the stove.

"Wayne what did I tell you?" she said.

"Your sister is my girlfriend, Wayne. We're going to get married so you might want to get to know your brother-in-law instead of acting all crazy. I'm sure that you'll find me to be the kind of nigga you'd like dealing with," Brick said. Resha was shocked. She just stood there looking at the both of them. She never expected for Brick to say that they were getting married. She thought about it briefly, maybe it was time to marry again. Was Brick serious? He couldn't be, they had just met. Maybe he was being sarcastic.

"Married, huh? That's good. At first I thought you was just one of them niggas out preying on lonely women. You know one of them dog ass niggas trying to hit something and run. I may have been wrong, but I still don't know yet, you might be trying to fool me and if that's the case you got another thing coming. I'm kind of a hard fool," Wayne said putting on his best smile.

"There's one thing I'm not my nigga you can bet your ass on it and that's a con man. I'm in these streets because that's what I do, but I ain't out to use nobody. That shit has a way of coming back on you," Brick said taking a bite of his chicken. He was waiting on Wayne to respond.

"So what do you do?" Wayne asked, he was curious. He had seen how Brick was riding. He figured Brick was slanging.

"What you mean?" Brick said.

"You know what I mean, bruh...what you do for a living? You know, how do you make your money and don't tell me that you work at Mac Donald's because I ain't buying that. I seen the whip and you look like you got money so keep it real. You selling that snow, huh?" Wayne asked.

"Man, you wired up or something? You sound like a fed," Brick said laughing. Resha dismissed herself from the kitchen.

"I guess it really just depends, I guess I do all kinds of stuff. I'm like a jack of all trades you feel me?" Brick said.

"So can you get your hands on some snow like a brick?" Wayne asked.

Brick laughed, "What makes you think that I have to get my hands on it...what makes you think that I don't have it now?"

"I mean, you may... I don't know that's why I'm asking you. My man is trying to cop something and his money is good, but he can't find a plug that keeps it. Every nigga that we run into runs out," Wayne said.

"I don't know, man. I don't know your nigga...how do I know that he's straight?" Brick asked.

"Man you've seen him before...Mike, the nigga in the white Camaro. We was together the first time that I ever saw you," Wayne said.

"Yea I remember who you're talking 'bout. Tall cat, look like he should be in the NBA, he hustles huh?...What he paying?" Brick asked swallowing the last of his mac and cheese.

"It depends sometimes as cheap as eighteen G's, but his man Bobby ain't had none lately. Somebody jacked him and now he talking some crazy numbers like twenty five. Nigga got to be smoking, it ain't that high in New York," Wayne said.

"Look, I don't really know your boy Mike and that ain't how I like to do business you feel me because niggas on shit out here. I don't trust myself half the time so if I do this I'll be doing it for you. I see y'all working together and I want to see y'all young cats get money for real. You said Bobby was giving it to you for like eighteen? I guess that's good. I can beat them numbers though if you shop with me. I'll make sure you eat out here...I'm talking like sixteen nigga. Solsa price all brick no shake," Brick said rubbing his palms and nodding his head.

"Damn that's what I'm talking about, so how soon can you get us one?" Wayne asked standing up from the table.

"I ain't finish lil nigga. And since you're my future brother-n-law, this first one is fifteen and I ain't just talking…I got it in the car with me right now," Brick said. Resha walked back into the room. she had a smile on her face. You could tell she was happy to see the two of them getting along.

"So how did you like the food Brick? I mean I could of threw down, but I was pressed for time," Resha said. It had been so long since she had cooked for a man. It felt good and brought back memories.

"Aw baby if you could have done better than that I'm scared. That was too good," he said licking his fingers. Wayne had just gotten off his cell phone.

"Good news, bruh. He wants it and he's waiting…about how long do you think it would take us to get to the carwash on Gallatin Road…I'm riding with you," Wayne said.

"Aww in that case, no time, we're in a Cutlass, baby."

CHAPTER 11

F YOU PAY ME!!!

"Man I've been trying to reach you...you've been hard to get in touch with lately...what are you doing running for president? I'm telling you now, you ain't getting my vote nigga," Foot said into the phone. He was at the Maxwell hotel downtown enjoying the view and trying to get his thoughts together.

"Naw not quite, son. I've been in Miami for the past few days taking care of business because that's what men do. They pay to play or they're swept away," Cain broke out into an uncontrollable laugh.

"You feel me my nigga?" He continued to laugh. Something wasn't right. Foot could feel it.

"I guess. What was that suppose to mean? In a slick way I feel like you just threatened me...I may be wrong, but that's what it sound like to me," Foot said. Who did this nigga think he was? Foot was using his wild card. Cain was acting kind of weird. Maybe Low Don was behind the hit, he still owed him money, but that didn't make sense. The Don understood business and he was fair, besides Foot made

Low a lot of money and it didn't make sense to want him dead. Cain cleared his voice.

"First of all let's get one thing straight...Cain don't make threats he makes money, he makes reservations and every now and then he even makes bond, but a threat is beneath me," he paused and inhaled a line of powder off of a plate that he had in front of him and tilted his head back.

"So you got that paper or what?" Cain asked.

Foot had an idea.

"As a matter of fact I do. Well not all of it, but I will in a few hours. Things done picked up on this end so go ahead and get ready and I'll be calling you back in a little bit...Oh and tell Low that I said that I'm sorry that it took so long, but I'm sending something extra with you to show my appreciation. And hey Cain, no hard feelings my man. I just got a lot on my mind so forgive me," Foot said. Suddenly it was a knock on Foot's hotel door. He disconnected the phone and headed to the door taking his time dragging his Prada flip flops. The knock continued.

"Who is it?...I don't need anything." Foot opened the door to find Bobby standing there.

119

"Damn it took you long enough. I was expecting to see you last night," Foot said fastening the belt on his silk robe.

"You mean this morning? Bruh it was about five when you called me and some of us do sleep. Besides you didn't say 'come now it's an emergency, so I thought I'd get the rest of my sleep. I see you're still alive, that's good. Now can I come in or are you going to make me stand in the hall all day, at least give me a chair damn," Bobby said.

"Come on in, my bad, bruh. I'm not all here at the moment so excuse me," Foot said heading back to the bed.

"Yea it sho looks nice up in here, so this is how the ballers spend their time?" Bobby said looking around. There seemed to be mirrors everywhere and the finest wood, not to mention the view. You could see clean across town from the bed. Bobby took a seat at the bar.

"Don't mind if I do," he said picking up a bottle of Champaign from the ice. "I didn't know that you was an alcoholic," Bobby said.
"I'm not it comes with my suite," Foot said turning the plasma on to ESPN.

"Oh I see you're still fly as ever," Bobby said. He envied Foot, but in a good way.

Secretly he was his role model, but he would never tell him that. It was some things a man had to keep to himself.

"Since you mentioned it you don't look too bad yourself. So what's your secret nigga? You slangin' bricks on the low?" Foot asked jokingly.

"Hell I wish...It's hard out here. I'm looking for an old lick myself...I'm not used to this. I've been thinking about selling my truck," Bobby said.

"I'm afraid your truck ain't going to pay me my nigga. Hell you can sell a hundred trucks and still be short with the interest and all. Hell you already owe me what..... three to four million," Foot said.

Bobby couldn't tell if he was joking or not.

"Come on, bruh. Interest, are you serious? I'm on your side," Bobby said laughing hoping that Foot would show some kind of humor, finally he smiled then frowned again.

"I know and I want to believe you Bobby I really do, but you make it hard," Foot said glancing at his Jacob watch. Time seemed to be moving pretty slow.

"What are you talking about, bruh?" Bobby asked.

"Well for starters the next time that you think I'm stressed and need to let my hair down just let me deal with it because I took your advice and I went to the sports bar, had a nice time, I met a lady and everything. As soon as I leave the bar and stops for gas there was a guy hanging by the pumps, you know like they always do. He asked could he pump and I said yea. When he finished he comes to my window and I gives him a five dollar bill so he tried to sell me some CDs. I'm checking out what he got then he goes in his bag, pulls out an Uzi then says something about the 'same thang that I had last time'. I smashed, he sprayed the car and blew out the back window only missing me by inches but scared the hell out of the lady. And now I doubt that I'll ever see her again, you talk about a hell of a night," Foot said taking a deep breath. He'd been through worse shit, but not in such a short time.

"Did you recognize the nigga?" Bobby asked puzzled.

"How could I when he was dressed like a bum? I couldn't have Id'ed him in a line up if I had to to save my life," Foot said.

Bobby just sat there and listened. It seemed like yesterday they were on top of the world and now all of a sudden things had taken a turn for the worse. Bobby kind of felt sorry for Foot. Hell even though he had been the one who was shot, but nobody was really trying to kill him. Hell he had only been shot as a message for Foot in the first place. He wished there was something that he could do to help, he felt like it was kind of his fault.

"Bruh, you know I'm with you one hundred percent…you can trust me," Bobby said.

"Nigga, I don't trust my momma, it's wicked out here and people change. Niggas stab you in the back, set you up to be killed then run off with your money and your bitch. It's cold out here. Everybody that I know done tried to play me one way or another. Folks don't seem to be happy unless I'm that beast." Foot slid his hand under a pillow and removed an all black Mac11 with a magazine that looked something like a walking cane.

"No more losses. I think I know who might be behind this. I got a plan," Foot said.

....

"Where's your homey? Said Brick. I thought you said he was waiting. See I'm not with this already, he got us sitting here like I'm the sell or something. Call that fool back and tell him if he want it he better be pulling up in the next 60 seconds or I'm gone and when he calls me back it's twenty five like Bobby." Brick was backed in on the side of the carwash next to a broken vacuum.

"How long he think I can pretend to be vacuuming the car?" Brick said pissed off. Suddenly the white Camaro pulled up and parked next to him. There were two people in the car, a bald headed fat nigga was driving and Mike was on the passenger side.

"What the hell is up with yo' boy? Didn't you tell him to come alone and he pulls up with some other nigga in the car. Aww naw tell him that's ok. I'm good...maybe some other time," Brick said. By that time Mike was opening the door getting into the back seat.

"Man sorry it took me so long I had to count the money again. I was trying to make sure everything was straight...feel me?" Mike said smiling.

"What's up with your homeboy in the car? I don't mean no harm, but that ain't how I rock so the next time come by yourself or ain't nothing...I thought Wayne told you that," Brick said.

"He probably did, but dude is like my pops, he's straight. I feel you man, my bad," Mike said.

Brick was watching Mike through his rearview mirror. He didn't like strange niggas sitting behind him, especially ones that he didn't know.

"It's in the glove box. Wayne just push that lil button right there on the door...you see it?" Brick asked.

Wayne did as he was told. The glove box opened and there it sat, one kilo still in the wrapper. Wayne and Mike was shocked. They had never saw that much dope at one time.

"Go head and buss it open if you want to, but it's real you can take my word for it. I'm straight 'bout business no games," Brick said passing the brick to Mike.

"No need my friend I believe you. Plus I ain't got time right now. I'll check it out when I get back to where I'm going," Mike said then suddenly Brick felt the feeling of cold steal on his neck.

"My boy this is a 45 trust me you won't make it. Now where is the rest of the dope at? Wayne get his strap, I know he got one." Wayne patted Brick's waist.

"Where's that strap at fool?" Wayne said.

"Aww we're doing it like this Wayne? Nigga I know we ain't doing it like this!" Brick said raising his voice.

"Shut up before I pop you nigga. I'm not finna keep asking you where that strap at either," Wayne said.

Brick could feel Mike pressing the gun against his neck even harder.

"It's under the seat," Brick mumbled. Wayne reached under the seat and grabbed Brick's 40 glock.

"Nice doing business with you," Mike said.

"Now pull up out of here and don't look back or we're bussin'...you're lucky that your rims won't fit on my Camaro or I would take your car too," Mike said. Wayne jumped in Mike's car and they sped off. Brick pulled off slowly, he couldn't believe that Resha's little brother had just robbed him. He picked up his phone and called Resha.

"Hello," Resha said answering the phone.

"You're not going to believe this because I barely can," Brick said.

"What's wrong? Is Wayne ok?" Resha yelled into the phone.

"Aww he is for now, but as soon as I catch him his ass is through. I'm sorry baby, but there's some shit that you just can't overlook. Him and his lil homeboy, Mike, just robbed me for a measly lil key that I was giving to them for almost free. I showed the lil nigga love and this is how he repays me. I'm on my way home now to get my chopper since they like playing with guns. Wait until they get a load of this," Brick said.

"Hold up Brick. I'm sorry baby, I really am, but let me try to talk to him first, let me get it back. Please don't kill my brother, please do this for me...let me call you right back. I'm going to call him right now hold on," the phone went dead in Brick's ear.

Sister or no sister somebody was going to pay for this." he called Justus.

"Where you at bruh? I just got robbed." Brick said.

"I'm at home...where you at? I'm on my way," Justus said.

"Naw stay at home. I'm around the corner from the house, I'll be pulling up in five minutes."

"Ha, ha, ha!" Justus laughed out loud. "So you let the lil punk get the ups on you? I bet your eyes almost popped out your head, make that face you just made again." Justus was cracking up. He had laughed so hard that tears were running out of his eyes, he could hardly see.

"Nigga you think it's funny, but it could have been you with a barrel on your neck and then I bet it wouldn't be as funny then, huh?" Brick was upset. He didn't think it was funny at all.

"Aww the baby is mad. Cheer up bruh, it's just dope and this is what I was telling your ass anyway ...all of this comes with the territory. Bird man want to be a baller nigga. You better get used to having guns on your head, niggas hungry out here and they'll eat their momma," Justus said slapping his clip into his glock 40 and stuffing it on his waist.

"I'm going to punish this lil nigga. Resha just going to have to be mad but I can't let this shit ride," Brick said. "Every nigga and they momma would be trying to test me."

"So what you think she gone do when you kill her lil brother? You say he's all she got," Justus said trying to talk some sense into Brick's head.

"I don't know what she gone do all I know is..." Suddenly his cell phone rang, it was Resha's number.

"Hello," Brick answered.

"Baby, I talked to Wayne," she said.

"What did he say?" Brick asked. The waiting game was about to drive Brick crazy.

"I told him that if he didn't give it back I was through with him and he put up a fight, but he's bringing it over. The problem is that he sold some out of it, but he's bringing the money too and I think that he wants to apologize," she said.

"How soon can you come over?" Resha asked.

He thought to himself, so that's it? Nigga think he can just take my shit and give it back? Who in the hell does he think he is?

"How soon can we get over Reshas? Because that punk bringing my shit back," Brick asked Justus.

"Tell her we'll be there in a lil minute. Hold tight, first we need to swing by the park. Fatso's ready to see us, he said something about his boy is running low and if we want it come holla at him," Justus said.

"Resha baby, give us a minute. We got to take care of something, but I'm on the way,"

Brick said. Fatso was at the park waiting as usually.

Damn what was taking Justus and Brick so long? He had been waiting patiently for the past 15 minutes and still no sign of them nowhere. He stepped out of his truck and sat on his hood watching a couple of old ladies walk laps in the park. He thought about trying to walk a lap or two, but quickly changed his mind. It had been years since he had worked out, he was clearly out of shape and the last place that he wanted to die was at a park. He glanced back over his shoulder and saw Justus pulling up. He stood up off the hood and wiped the wrinkles out of his LRG jogging suit.

"Damn what took y'all so long? For a minute I thought y'all had got lost, I was just about to get my smash on. I told y'all that I was in a hurry," Fatso said.

"My bad something came up, we got here as quick as we could," Justus said throwing the duffle bag of money in the back of Fatso's truck.

Brick spoke up, "We brought everything, it's five hundred on the nose," Brick said smiling, he was feeling himself.

"You think we can get the hundred? You see the money good, we'll be ready in a week, a hundred plus fifty," Brick asked.

"Aww that's what I meant to tell you, I don't got it on me this time. The police was hot, they kind of spooked me, but I got it down the street at my spot. Y'all can stay here while I run and go get it or y'all can head back to the house. I'll pull up on y'all in about 20 minutes," Fatso said getting back into his truck. "Oh yea I won't take all day like y'all did. My beard almost turned gray." They all laughed.

"Yea just call my phone when you're ready, we'll be in the neighborhood," Justus said. Suddenly a thought entered his mind. He quickly dismissed it, they had trusted Fatso with all they were worth, but he was loyal. He could be trusted.

All brick no shake…

CHAPTER 12

GRACE AVE!!!

Grace Avenue was one of Nashville's busiest streets. You could tell by the rush of traffic that this neighborhood was all but peaceful. Flashy cars scattered the streets, loud music and beer bottles. Snitch watch was in full effect and if you dug in your nose somebody knew about it. A community center sat on the hill, a rest haven for all the drugs pushers and thugs. Why Cain wanted to meet here no one knows. It was 90 degrees outside and the police were probably hotter. Foot and Bobby sat parked in front of the center.

"Man I still don't know bruh. It just don't make no sense for Low Don to be trying to whack you and on top of that you would think he needs you. Do you know how much coke we push in a week?...that would be like cutting off one of your own arms or you killing me. It just don't make sense." Bobby had been playing Sherlock Holmes and as hard as he tried, this was one puzzle he couldn't figure out. He rolled the window down and took a glance across the street. A gray STS crept slowly into the parking lot.

"Hey what you say that fool was driving? Is that him?" Bobby asked.

"Yea that's him. The nigga kind of shaky so you stay cool. I'll be right back." Foot reached under the seat and removed his Mac cocking it to make sure one was in the chamber. He stuffed it in his pants the best he could without the clip being to noticeable and stepped out the car walking swiftly toward Cain's STS. Cain was laid back on the soft leather surrounded by wood grain listening to Al Green. When Foot opened the door and stepped inside, Cain didn't appear to be happy to see him at all.

"It took you long enough, where's the bread?" he said looking straight ahead as if looking directly at Foot would somehow drain his power.

"Damn that's no way to talk to a friend. You didn't even give me a chance to ask how was your day or what did you eat for lunch...what seems to be the problem?" Foot asked. He knew that he was eating at Cain's patience. Cain maintained his focus.

"You're the problem, Foot. Punks like you are the problem. You hog the damn streets and think that everybody supposed to fear you. Then you meet good niggas like Low and you try to play up under them acting like you're their friend when you're really a snake.... unworthy of even standing beside a gangster as real as Low. I don't even know what the hell he see in you honestly. I'm the one taking all the chances, I should be running the ball not you," Cain said. For a minute silence filled the air and you could hear a pin drop.

"Naw you wrong, nigga. I'm not no snake just a real nigga and real recognize real, you on the other hand are a hater. I thought I read you right a long time ago," Foot said.

"Hater never, but you are a dead man." Suddenly Cain removed an all black 357 from under his shirt, Foot's mind went racing. Thinking fast he reached for the gun. Cain was strong. Foot struggled to keep the gun pointed away from him, he twisted Cain's arm causing him to drop the gun, but not before discharging the bullet, but it went through the door. With his right hand Foot grabbed the gun.

"You won't get away this time!" Cain yelled.

Bobby was unaware of what was going on until he heard the "Boom!" followed by, "Boom! Boom!" The whole car seemed to light up as if it were a firework show on the 4th of July. Then he heard it again, "Boom! Boom!" unclear of what was going on, he dashed from the car. Foot was in trouble, he thought, until he saw Foot leap from the STS caring a duffle bag heading straight for him.

"Man it was a setup, it was that fool all along and I doubt that Low even knew...get in the car push that bitch ass nigga over and follow me. We can't leave his car here the police will be here any minute!" Foot yelled.

Bobby hesitated. He didn't want to ride in the car with a dead man. How in the hell would he explain that to the police if they were to stop him for some strange reason.

"Why I got to drive the car?" Bobby asked. "How about you drive the S and I'll follow you in your car?" Bobby replied.

"Because I said so!" Foot yelled and for a split second Foot saw what he should have never seen in Bobby's eyes. He saw fear and fear was never a friend, a scared man would get you and himself a hundred years.

"Ok" Bobby said and jogged to Cain's car.

"Hey Bobby!" Foot yelled.

Bobby turned around only to find Foot aiming his Mac directly at him.

"What are you doing?" Bobby screamed, he saw death in Foot's eyes. He'd seen that look before and knew it all too well.

"You never were built like me, you got a soft spot Bobby and only the strong survives," Foot said pulling the trigger. The Mac exploded sending a shower of hot led all over Bobby's body lifting him off his feet and slamming him hard onto the concrete. Foot hopped into his car and sped off. From a distance he could hear sirens wail. He ran a stop sign at the end of the street causing an old lady in a gray station wagon to swerve to avoid hitting him, you could see the old lady's mouth moving, and she appeared to be cursing him out. Foot adjusted his speed to the flow of traffic and turned off onto a side street. Finally he could breathe; he was safe and rich again. That's one less nigga to leach off of him. It's a cold world, he thought to himself. He wanted to cry, but his success wouldn't allow it. Then he saw lights which appeared to be everywhere. Your boy is a star or either this is all a bad dream. Suddenly the road block snapped him back to reality and the sight of cops aiming guns directly at him made it all so clear. He slowed the car down and put it in reverse only to find himself blocked in from the back also and from a distance he could hear a helicopter in the sky.

"Damn this couldn't be happening!" he searched the streets for ways to escape, but it was no use, they had him surrounded. A police officer yelled through a bull horn, "Step out of the car with your hands up, we have you surrounded...I repeat hands up!" At that moment Foot saw his whole life flash before his eyes. He remembered when he was just a youth sitting on his father's lap smelling the alcohol on his breath and listening to him talk. He remembered hearing him say, "Man is supposed to be free, jail ain't even for the birds and before I go back I'll go to the grave. Fuck the police." It was then that he made up his mind. Stepping out of the car slowly he aimed his Mac at the cops. Some took cover as he fired blindly injuring two officers and killing another instantly. Foot never saw it coming, never saw his killer only felt the slug rip the back of his head in half as he dropped to his knees, eyes open!!!

CHAPTER 13

Honey I'm Home!!!

Knock, knock, knock! The oak wood door sounded off like a mini drum. Resha made her way through the living room almost falling over a chair that was in the way. "I'm coming baby." She unlocked the door opening it quickly.

"Sorry it took me so long, boo," she said and then gasped for air as the gun touched her forehead. Lil Darrel pushed his way inside the house.

"Have a seat we'll make this quick as possible," he said locking the door behind him. Darrel was a twisted freak and he knew it, it didn't bother him at all. At times he frightened himself, he considered himself to be a real nightmare on Elm Street.

Resha was terrified. She had never had a gun pointed at her before or been robbed, but she knew that any wrong move could get her killed.

"My purse is in the bedroom, please don't kill me!" she said shaking. Darrel threw her on the couch. For a minute she wanted to scream, but decided not to instead she began to cry.

"Don't cry yet. I'm just getting started...Do you know why I'm here? Where are they?" Darrel asked as he reached back and slapped Resha across the face with his 9 millimeter. She felt one of her teeth chip as blood flowed from her mouth. She didn't know what the hell he was talking about. She managed to say between sobs, "I'm here by myself and I live by myself...who are you looking for?" she asked nervously. Darrel began to smile. He could see that the lady was frightened and this aroused him.

"I'll ask all the questions, let's get that straight. I would hate to see your pretty little face all messed up so listen closely...I want you to call Justus and Brick and tell them to get here ASAP. If they ask is there a problem you tell them no you just have something that you need to talk about and it's kind of important. No funny shit or you can kiss this nice house goodbye," Darrel said.

Resha picked up her cell phone, nervously she dialed Brick's number slowly. She hoped that he would be able hear in her voice that something was wrong. The phone rang twice and he answered, "Hey baby girl," he said.

"Hey Brick, do you think that you could come by here for a second? I really need to talk to you about something it's important," Resha said.

"What's wrong, boo? Did you forget that I'm on my way over there? We're like two streets over now I'll be pulling up in a second. Is everything ok?" Brick asked. He could sense that something was terribly wrong.

"All yea everything is cool I just need to talk to you so hurry up ok?" Resha said.

"Alright," Brick said then the line was disconnected.

"What did he say?" Darrel asked.

"He's on the way they're just a couple of streets over and they should be pulling up any minute now," Resha said.

"Perfect," Darrel said then quickly he tried phoning Bobby, but the phone just kept ringing. Suddenly there was a knock on the door. Darrel took cover in the kitchen.

"Answer that and remember what I said, no funny shit or everybody gets it," Darrel said waiving his pistol.

Resha slowly unlocked the door then Justus and Brick walked in.

"Hey baby what's on your mind? You seemed worried on the phone. I got here as quick as I could." Brick hugged Resha.

"There's a man in the kitchen with a gun," Resha whispered in his ear, but by then it was too late. Darrel stepped out of the kitchen aiming his 9 millimeter.

"Greetings friends, I'm glad that you could make it. For a minute I was starting to get worried, I didn't know if you had gotten stuck in traffic or what. And sorry for being so rude, but umm, no tea just me. And if anybody move I'm popping it off so try me and die...I'm sure you've heard how I get down. Hold your hands up and turn around." Justus and Brick both did as they were instructed. Darrel searched them both and removed their weapons; they were both carrying twin glock 40s.

"Man, this was too easy. I'm going to mess around and get OG status for this. Brick the thug and Justus the ghost nigga. I don't know how y'all survived that hurricane last time. I don't usually hit the wrong people my aim is kind of good," Darrel laughed.

Justus heart almost jumped out of his chest. He couldn't believe what he was hearing. Maybe his mind was playing tricks on him. Is this the fool that killed his mother? It couldn't be, but from the looks of it he had come back to finish his job. Justus had never felt so helpless in his life, he was starting to hear voices. Something kept telling him, "You can take him." But he had sense enough to know that was stupid. One mistake and he would be buried next to his mother.

"What do you want?" Justus asked.

"You know damn well what I want nigga...I want Foot's money back that y'all took from Bobby. I'm sure that you remember that, those bricks and that money fool," Darrel said angrily pointing his pistol back and forth from Brick to Justus.

"So why did you kill my mother coward?" Justus said not caring if his words offended the gunman. Darrel looked at Justus in his eyes and laughed that insane laugh that only he could do so well.

"My friend there's casualties in war," Darrel said.

Wayne couldn't believe his ears, he had been glued to the door for the last couple of minutes, something was definitely wrong. And from the sounds of it his sister was in trouble. He had known from the very second that he pulled up that there were too many cars in the yard and Resha hardly ever had company. The gray dodge Ram looked familiar, it was something about it that spelled trouble. He had to think fast and his sister needed him and no way would he let her down.

"Mike you go around the back, there's a door to the kitchen and it's usually open so that I can get in. Just turn the knob slowly to the left and on the count of ten we're going in. Na' make that the count of five and look nigga don't shoot me," Wayne said and Mike took off.

Wayne began to count and by the time he reached four his whole body was soak and wet like he had jumped into a pool. He raised his leg high as his foot struck the target "Boom!" sending the whole door tumbling off the hinges. He stepped in with his 40 aimed directly at the man holding the gun, Mike was behind him.

Darrel swung around like a soldier in the army with great skills. He fired hitting Mike in the shoulder causing him to drop his weapon. It's was then that Wayne fired, "Boom! Boom!" The slugs sent Darrel spinning like a top and screaming out in agony as he dropped to one knee and fell over on his back moaning. Wayne stepped closer, ready to finish him off. He had never killed anyone before, but he was sure that he could.

"No! Justus screamed picking up his glock off the table. "This one is on me." He strolled over to Darrel's moaning body, he was moving as if he was trying to crawl away. Justus took his foot and kicked him in the mouth repeatedly until his blood and teeth were on the floor and covering his shoes.

"You ain't so tough now are you killer? You bitch!" Justus said kneeling down. He placed his glock in Darrel's mouth and squeezed, "Boom!" Brain matter stained the carpet as Justus stood there looking. "Eye for an eye killer!" Justus shouted and fired another round into his lifeless head. "Alright let's get this mess cleaned up...Resha where are the garbage bags? Let's get this trash up out of here, bleach it up and wipe it down...Do you think that the neighbors called the cops?" Justus asked.

Resha was in shock. She tossed Brick some bags. "Naw the closest neighbors are out of town, but move fast just in case," she said. Resha was playing doctor on Mike's shoulder luckily the bullet had gone straight through. She patched it and wrapped it the best she could. It would do until he made it to a hospital. Brick stood there face to face with Wayne for the first time since the robbery.

"Wayne the hero," Brick said.

"Hey look..." Wayne began, "man I'm sor..."

Brick interrupted him, "Hold up not yet give me my gun first," Brick said.

Wayne smiled and passed Brick the gun then suddenly Brick swung striking Wayne in the mouth knocking him flat on his ass.

"Man what was that for?" Wayne said holding his mouth.

"That was for that stunt you pulled nigga. Don't ever bite the hand that feeds you. If your lil homeboy Mike wasn't already shot, I'd pop a nice hole in his ass, but he's hurt enough. Now we can squash it," Brick said extending his hand out to help Wayne up off the floor.

"Now where's my money?" Brick asked.

"It's in the car," Wayne said.

"Give it to your sister and I want you to sell the rest of that work and give it to your sister also because after today I think that she may want to move and if not it's still hers...you understand?" Brick asked.

"Yea I can dig it," Wayne said then he thought to himself that Brick may not be so bad after all. He seemed to really care about Resha and that was a good thing, most niggas were selfish.

Justus was busy dragging the jumbo trash bag with the body to the back door. "Here." he tossed Wayne Darrel's truck keys. "Pull the truck around to the back and help me load this mess then take the truck down to the tracks and torch it. Make sure you wipe it down, no finger prints...you hear me?" Justus asked.

145

Wayne moved quickly. "Got you boss," Wayne said jokingly.

"Mike you follow him in Resha's car to make sure that he gets back safe," Justus said.

"Got it," Mike said. He was in pain, but he had felt worse. Once he had been shot in the stomach... now that hurt. They loaded the truck and Wayne pulled off with Mike tailing him.

"The lil nigga ain't bad after all," Brick said hugging Resha. "It's going to be alright baby, I promise. This is just one of those crazy things that happens in this crazy ol' world," Brick said. They laughed and for a minute they escaped this crazy ol' world.

Justus walked out of the kitchen and tossed Brick the telephone. The look on his face told it all, but the operator made it all so clear, "The number you have dialed has been disconnected." This couldn't be happening, that nigga Fatso had pulled a fast one over on them. He ran off with everything they owned. Brick dialed the number again, but received the same message. The nerve of that nigga, you just can't trust anybody these days. Fatso was a dead man. He can't run forever, Brick swore to himself. The sound of someone knocking snapped him back into reality. They had tried to fix the door the best they could, but you could still see through the crack.

"Damn it's the police," Brick said. "Just be cool." He collected the straps and ran toward the back of the house to hide the guns in a pile of dirty clothes then came back to the living room and seated himself on the couch.

"Answer the door, see what they want and just be cool," Brick said. Justus couldn't believe it. Something had told him to get low an hour ago, now the damn cops were outside.

Resha opened the door. "Yes officer, how may I help you?" Resha asked in her politest voice, the officer appeared to be in his early twenties and he was wearing a hat that said 'Sheriff' in his hand was a piece of paper.

"Excuse me madam. I'm sorry to bother you, but I'm looking for a Brad Cowan. I have a warrant here for an aggravated assault on a Ms. Shawn Lillard and I was told that I could find him here," the sheriff said.

Brick shot up from the couch, "I'm Brad Cowan, but I haven't assaulted anybody," Brick said. The officer looked at Brick, "I'm sorry mister, but if you would please come with me I'm sure we could get this all worked out," he said. That little slut, Brick thought. She done took a warrant out on me? The officer was becoming impatient so Brick allowed himself to be handcuffed and arrested. Shawn had the nerve to pull some shit like this. He wondered how in the hell she had known Resha's address and better yet how did Darrel?

"Aww baby you gone be ok. I'm here for you, I promise." Resha was trying to comfort Brick as best she could. Her and Justus escorted him to the officer's patrol car and watched him get in.

"I'm on my way downtown bruh, don't panic. You good, it could be worse. Remember that," Justus said and he was damn right. Brick smiled.

Two weeks later at C.J.C county jail visitation, Resha and Justus sat at the table waiting for Brick to be brought out. The judge had denied his bond because Shawn said that she had feared for her life. Truth was she just couldn't stand to see him with somebody else. He took a cop out for six months, two for one, which meant that he wouldn't serve any more than 3 months. Although he was pissed off he accepted it. After all it could have been worse. Brick hugged Resha and sat at the table.

"My main man you don't look so bad in orange although I must admit freedom is much better," Justus said. The two of them laughed.

Brick had had enough of jail. He was ready to get back to the money.

"Man I hate jail already. They feed us bologna every day and it's green. I'm not trying to eat that shit, it be done gave me Mad Cow or something. Did you put that money on my books for me? Store is Friday and you don't want your boy falling off in here do you?" Brick said raising his shirt showing Justus his rib cage sucking his stomach in.

"You better know it, Resha dropped one too. Resha was in a daze. She hadn't taken her eyes off of Brick since he had strolled out. She was falling for him and there wasn't anything that she wouldn't do for him.

"Oh, about that business that I was telling you on the phone... sorry that I couldn't talk freely because the calls are monitored. What I was trying to tell you was that you never would believe who I share a cell with." Brick looked around the visitation room as if he alone was being watched. He spoke in a whisper, "Cash, Cash Johnson, Low Don's brother. Can you believe that shit? Low is supplying the whole state, but here is the good news: Cash had heard what happened to us and said that Fatso had been shopping with them. He popped up with a half of a mill bragging about how he just had got over on some niggas. He was heading for Chicago and a day later he called from jail saying that he had been jammed with the money in an ecstasy bust."

Justus nodded his head as he listened. They had worked so damn hard for that money and in the blink of an eye it was gone. Now some crooked ass police would enjoy his blood sweat and tears.

"Damn in the back of my mind I was still hoping to catch that nigga." Justus massaged his temples and took a deep breath.

"One thing is for sure, Fatso better play dead. If he ever showed his face again. There would be no exception..."so what's up with this 'Cash' nigga...what he talking?" Justus asked.

"Dig this, he said that he could hook us up with Low... possibly front us with some more work to put us back in the game. He said Low's main workers just got popped and he was looking for some real niggas to fill their shoes. Think about it, with Low Don supplying us, Foot dead, ain't no limit to the paper we could stack, we would own the city." As Brick talked Justus took it all in and weighed the options. Foot had gotten smoked in a shootout with the police. It was either sign on or sign off. Who wanted to be broke? He had already become accustomed to the high life, nice whips, expensive clothes, hot chicks that couldn't seem to keep their hands off of them. Money made everything better and lots of it made everything great. Fuck being nobody, the choice was simple.

"Look here man. I heard about this Low Don nigga, he's a straight killer who buries niggas alive about his money. I heard the feds once had him under investigation for drug trafficking and their main witness popped up in the dessert in Arizona, well his head did. They still haven't found his body. With nobody left to testify they gave up, well actually the DA vanished so the judge decided to back the fuck off. I don't blame him. If we take his shit you know what that means?"

"What?" Brick asked.

"We get him his money by all means. No fucking around, loyalty is everything, deal?"

Brick extended his hand across the table to shake on it indicating that he was serious, a kool-aid smile stretched across his face. "Deal," he said. He was ready to get back to work. As soon as he got back to his cell, he informed Cash that it was all good. Now all that was left to do was to get out. His last week seemed to go by in slow motion, but when it finally arrived there was no stopping it. Home sweet home...

Resha had put together a surprise party welcoming him back. Somehow she had convinced his momma to go along with it. When he walked through the door of Resha's house, everyone yelled "Surprise!" He was shocked to see his aunt Helen and his uncle Mat. His sister Lisa had come in from Atlanta, her and her husband and they had even brought his nieces and nephews. There were a few faces that he didn't recognize, but what the hell it was the thought that counted. Justus was the only true friend that he had ever had. Every other nigga that came around was there for a reason. The music was loud, Resha had made Brick's cake from scratch... his favorite caramel and chocolate. There were hot wings, lobster tails, steak, fish, pizza, several different types of cheese and every drink that you could imagine.

"Boy I'm glad to see you made it up out that place in one piece...you still got all your marbles, don't you? That ain't no place for a man. I wouldn't wish it on my worst enemy," Uncle Mat said on his fourth Heineken. His forehead had begun to sweat, it always did that when he was half way tipsy, which was all the time.

"Hell Unk, I was only in there for a few weeks. I hope that I still got all of my marbles. Actually it wasn't all that bad. I did a lot of thinking while I was in there, I even came out with something that I didn't have before I went in." Brick was thinking about his new connect, but of course he couldn't tell his Uncle Mat that so he said, "It was truly a learning experience." Brick signaled for Resha to turn the radio down. When she did he said, "Look, I want to thank everyone for coming out to support me. This is truly a day that I'll never forget. Family is important and you all mean everything to me, believe it or not I wish that I got to see you more often…Auntie I love you baby, you're as beautiful as ever. Sis you've always been the better one, don't follow me," he said laughing. "I love you all." And there it was she had finally heard it, it was music to her ears. She melted inside and it was at that moment she knew that she loved him too…

CHAPTER 14

All About Cash

Cash had been released from the county jail two days before Brick and as always he kept his promise. It was a beautiful day; the sun was shining as if it had something to prove, the sky was a soft aqua blue not a rain cloud for miles. One of the reasons Cash had his top down; the other reason was that he liked to show off his interior. It had cost him a fortune just like the car Bugatti grand sport, sixteen cylinders, one thousand horse power kept him exhaling air like a dragon blowing steam. Since he loved speed it was his favorite. On the weekend he pushed an all black on black Aston Martin V8 Vantage. He had cash no doubt. The meeting spot was PF Changs on West End Ave. Only ballers ate there, it was the perfect place to negotiate. Cash sat at his table waiting for Brick and Justus to arrive while he played with his I-Phone. He was addicted to Twiiter and FaceBook. He met some of his best clientele online although the internet was dangerous; sometimes the feds posed as drug dealers trying to snag dummies who couldn't tell the difference. Cash could smell a cop a mile away. He had never served an undercover. He lasted years in the streets. His family supplied several cities and the only thing that he had on his record was a DUI and a few speeding tickets. His last ticket had cost him 30 days in jail. The judge was tired of seeing him, not even money could save him.

Justus and Brick walked through the door 15 minutes late, this aggravated Cash. Cash was a business man who prided himself on being prompt. He'd never been late for shit. Who did these niggas think they were? He didn't like their style already. Brick was too flashy; he sported a pair of big ass Dolce Gabbana shades and matching watch, his chains hung low, as a matter of fact he had on too many damn necklaces. All that jewelry shit was for Mister T, he'd have to have a talk with him about that, that shit draws the police like honey draws bees. He stood up from the table and greeted them both as they approached and shook their hands before sitting back down. When they were all seated he said, "Glad you boys could make it, for a moment I thought you boys had got lost. You're late...my time is valuable, don't waste it." Glancing at his Movado series 800, he signaled for a waiter and ordered a Kahlua on the rocks.

"Well let's get down to business, shall we?" Cash said smiling showing a set of pearly whites. His dentist had done wonders considering the shape that his teeth were in after having a mouth full of platinum removed. A reminder of his childish days. Now he was a grown man getting his grown man on.

"There's been a slight problem, but nothing we can't handle. I know that I told you that I could get you in and the offer is still good. I ran it by Low like I told you I would. I'm a man of my word. He's willing to give you guys a try." Brick and Justus listened attentively. "But first you must do him a favor."

Justus interrupted, "What is it?"

"Sure anything," Brick said. He wasn't about to let this once in a life time opportunity walk away no matter what the favor was. Justus would just have to trust him on this.

"Good. I was hoping that you said that. Tomorrow afternoon there's a shipment of pure Columbian cocaine coming in at the dock of Percy Priest. Originally it belonged to someone who had an unfortunate accident. Jesus will be expecting Dame, of course he will never show, instead you will. Be there to intercept the package and meet me at this address at two o'clock. Make sure you're not followed," Cash said scribbling the address on a small piece of paper. He slid it across the table.

"Piece of cake," he said. Brick thought so, too.

Justus had come too far to turn around now. I mean, how hard could it possibly be, he thought. "I'm in," he said.

Cash smiled. "Then we have a deal." He stood to shake their hands again before leaving. He had business to attend to and women to see. On his way out he turned and said, "And gentleman don't be late, Low would never forgive you. Our appointment is at 2:00 at 2:15 you're dead men. No exceptions. Chow.

CHAPTER 15

PAY DAY

Two Hispanic men unloaded the boat at the dock, another stood guard with an M16 hung from his shoulder. They spoke in Spanish, Brick and Justus watched from a safe distance. They could tell by the hand gestures that one of the men was making that something was wrong, he appeared to be angry. As soon as the last package was unloaded, they sprang into action crotched down low. They crossed the dock through a gap in the railing. They watched the guard smoke a cigarette and by the time he noticed Justus up on him, it was too late. He swung around in an attempt to raise the M16, the burst from Justus' Mac10 stopped him dead in his tracks. Two bullets entered his chest and one pierced his throat. Blood squirted from his neck like a fountain, eyes opened wide he dropped to his knees. With his last strength he squeezed the trigger of the M16, bullets struck the dirt as he collapsed face down. Before the other two men had time to react, Brick yelled, "On the ground, let me see your hands!" The men seemed to have understood English perfectly. Arms spread wide, they buried their faces in the grass. One man carried a 44 revolver stuffed in the small of his back. Brick quickly removed it and tossed it into the water.

"Do you motherfuckers speak English?" Brick asked aiming his Tec.

"Yes," one of the men answered.

"Good. We want that coke. Is this all of it? Is there anymore left on the boat?" Brick asked.

"No amigo, no more. Have it it's yours," he replied.

"Damn right it's ours!" Justus yelled. Suddenly the engine on the boat roared to life and the boat began to move quickly gaining speed.

"Stop that fucking boat! Somebody still on there! They're getting away!" Justus yelled.

Justus and Brick fired at the evading boat until their clips were empty then they quickly reloaded. When they turned around they were surprised to see the hostages fleeing toward the woods. They aimed and fired killing them instantly, the boat had manage to get away, but not before all the dope was unloaded. There it sat packaged in large crates so heavy it took the both of them to move one. There were six in total. They loaded them all in the back of a white moving truck that they had rented that morning from U-haul. Justus looked at his watch. It was 1:30 pm they had 30 minutes to get to Harding Place. That was plenty of time, as long as nothing freakish happened. They jumped onto the interstate heading north, just as the police swamped Percy Priest. The black 2013 Ford Taurus tailed the white moving truck at a safe distance. Traffic flowed smoothly. The driver accelerated just enough to keep up, occasionally switching lanes so as not to be detected. Approaching the Harding Place exit, the white truck veered to the right and got off the interstate, the Taurus followed. The driver picked up his two-way and pushed talk.

"Yea," a voice on the other end said.

"We're here...just got off the exit. They should be pulling up in a minute. Looks like they'll be early."

"Good so how did they handle it?" the voice on the other end said.

"Almost perfect. The driver of the boat got away as expected, but he'll be dead in thirty minutes."

"Good job."

"Thank you, sir."

Harding Ridge was home to some of the most famous people in Nashville; Tom Riddle the piano doctor, the legendary Ted Abernathy king of jazz, you name it. The trees were full of fruit, the grass even looked edible. Every house in the neighborhood was priced at least at a million dollars. It was truly a nice place to live. Minus the joggers and occasional cyclist, there was hardly ever anyone outside. So peaceful that it had been nicknamed, "The Garden of Eden," and besides the doctor next door, Cash was the only black person in the neighborhood. He stood at the door smiling while Justus and Brick unloaded the truck.

"In the kitchen and be careful. That's hundred thousand dollar tile," he said pointing to the floor.

"A hundred thousand dollar tile? This nigga is a bitch, no way in hell I'll spend a hundred g's on a floor," Justus thought.

They lined the crates up against the walls. Brick grabbed his back and wiped the sweat from his forehead. He exhaled and said, "Damn, this is the hardest I done worked in a long time."

Justus laughed and said, "Nigga this is the hardest I've worked ever."

"You guys did a great job. Low is proud of you and wants you to know that this is the beginning of a beautiful thing. We're going to make you niggas rich beyond your wildest dreams, you dig?" Cash said.

Justus and Brick nodded their heads, you could see the greed in their eyes.

"To show our appreciation Low's scheduling a get together tonight for the family staring you two. There will be bitches galore, Champaign and the best high-dro that you've ever seen in your life. We'll be downtown at the Maxwell House, Suite 225, no straps, no problems just family," Cash said opening the refrigerator. He grabbed a Mike's Hard Lemonade offering one to each of them. They drank in silence then Justus asked, "So how much shit is this anyway?" He had sold plenty of bricks before, but never seen enough to fill up a kitchen. Each crate had to hold at least 50 birds he was sure of that. Cash appeared shocked that he had asked. He walked over to one of the crates and removed the top.

"This here my friend is grade A 100% pure Columbian coca, each one of these crates holds 50 squares at 50%, that's 300 blocks times two...you do the math. This here my friend is what you call the mother lode." He smiled picking up one brick from the crate. He held it to his nose and smelled the wrapper. "Straight anthrax," he said placing the block back in the crate. Brick's mouth was opened so wide he could have easily inhaled a fly. His vision was blurred for a minute, all he could see were dollar signs. If only he had stumbled across that boat himself he could have rewrote history, the 21st century cocaine cowboys. Hell he could make Frank Lucas look like a hobo Wayne.

Justus was puzzled, he said, "You mean each one of these can be turned into two?"

"No I mean each one of these can be turned into whatever the fuck we want, but two is enough." They all laughed. Cash raised his bottle in the air. "This calls for a toast." They all raised they're bottles. "To the good life," Cash said.

"To the good life," Justus and Brick repeated...

CHAPTER 16

LOW DON

"Well one thing is for fucking sure, it appears to be drug related, it's over 75 shell cases over here," Sergeant Jones said squatting down pointing at every empty shell that he saw.

"I tell you the truth. Have you ever seen such damn brutality? These guys were chopped down like old weeds. Whoever done this must have hated them. From the looks of it they were trying to get away. Tag everything, I don't need that damn internal affairs breathing down my neck." Sergeant Jones was a vet, 350 pounds of true jelly rows with curly hair. He had been with the department for the last twenty years. He had survived two failed marriages and three gunshot wounds, he was one tough cookie. Officers teased that he'd be one hundred and twenty years old before he retired.

"Sir, take a look at this guy, he's the only one with ID. I ran his name through NCIC and this is what I came up with. It says here that he's Hernandez Martinez, if that's true this guy is Columbian Cartel. He's on the FBI's ten most wanted list. What the hell was he doing here?" Officer Dan Conway said scratching his head.

"Good question the FBI is gonna be all over this shit. I'm sure that they're on their way now...call it in," Sergeant Jones said.

"Pack it up boys we're out of here, this is someone else's pain in the ass."

The stretch Lincoln navigator SE arrived outside the Maxwell House just as expected. Ten swimsuit models exited and made their way up to Suite 225, the entire hotel had been closed down for the occasion. For the next 24 hours Low Don owned the building, invite only. The food had been prepared by some of the best chefs in the city. Everybody appeared to be having a great time as the music bumped with the women dancing. Cash was decked out in his Sean John original three piece suit, platinum cuff links and alligator flats, his presidential Rolex's blinged as the light shined off the princess cut bagget diamonds. Low Down was draped in an Armani jogging suit. You could tell he had exquisite taste, although tonight he sported tennis shoes. They all set together at the table, Low's right hand man Killer, his nephew Major, the twins Eric and Derrick and Quack the gun slinger. They had all come up from the sand box together. The newest addition to the family was Justus and Brick.

"Believe me when I say you two niggas are the luckiest niggas in the world tonight, it's not every day that I bless niggas with my presence. I must admit that I was surprised. When Cash first told me about you cats, I wasn't so sure. I hear you're about money that's all that matters. That shit that happened between y'all and Fatso... that's y'all shit, leave me out of it. The type of money that y'all are about to make now will make y'all forget them peanuts, trust me," Low said nodding his head. Everybody at the table seemed to all nod at once like puppets being controlled by strings. Killer was the average due boy, you could tell by the way he giggled every time Low said something that was half funny. He sported long dread locks dyed red at the tips. A want to be 'ladies man' whose only strength was his gun. Although he'd never killed anyone, he was convinced he was Charles Manson. Eric and Derrick were almost identical, they were both short, light-skinned and freckle faced. The only thing that set them apart was a tattoo that Derrick had on his neck that said 'Early', whatever that meant. Quack was the coolest of them all although serious about his paper, you could tell he didn't play no games. One of his eyes was cocked sideways. Although he wasn't blessed with good looks he made up for what he lacked in swagger.

"I run a tight shift, Twins work the Westside, Killer work the North, Cash runs the East, you two will get the South, so consider yourself as the replacements. Every nigga at this table is expendable, I won't take no shit believe me when I say it. We have a few rules that we live by... not many but a few. You will need to know these inside and out like the back of your hand...you following me?" Low waited until they had all responded before moving on.

"Rule one: don't fuck off my money, fuck off yours plain and simple. I want mines like the IRS...if my shit is short," he paused as if he had lost track of what he was saying then continued, "there will be extreme ramification...Rule two: don't fuck my bitch," he said pointing across the room at a chocolate beauty that was busy in conversation with another woman. "I don't give a fuck, if she's butt ass necked and you're drunk as Doc Holiday. I will Wyatt Earp you 'bout my bitch," he grinned, but you could tell by his tone that he was serious. "No snitching, no bitching and last, but not least: don't fuck with my bitch. Oh, I already said that, didn't I?" They all laughed. "Any questions?" Low asked.

"Yes I do have one as a matter of fact...how soon do we get started?" Brick asked. "Not that I'm in a hurry, but ain't nothing like being rich." Justus tossed his head back and laughed and gave Brick dap.

"Don't worry before you leave here tonight, you'll be loaded...there's a hundred a piece for both of you here now. In the morning you'll be driving two Silverados. They're parked in the parking garage and the keys are in the ignition. I suggest that you unload somewhere safe and have fun. You have a week to dump them. Welcome to the major league, but enough talk about business. Ladies, show these gentlemen a good time," he said motioning to two big booty strippers. They grabbed Justus and Brick by the hand and disappeared behind a door quickly...

CHAPTER 17

THE TAKE OVER!!!

"Brick, we need to talk," Resha said as he walked through her living room early the next day. He was still a bit hung over from all the liquor from the party. He'd been staying at Resha's house since he had been out of jail and Resha wanted to know where they now stood. She was in love with Brick and had given herself to him completely. As a matter of fact her period was late. She had made her an appointment to see a doctor in a few days, but that news would have to wait, maybe it was a false alarm. She doubted it though since she had experienced morning sickness for the past couple of days. Damn how could she allow herself to get in this situation? What if Brick wasn't ready to be a father? Or worse what if he wasn't ready to be in a committed relationship? The thought made her sick to her stomach, she instantly vomited missing the trashcan by a foot. She ran to the bathroom locking herself inside. Brick quickly followed. He turned the knob, but it didn't open.

"Baby what's wrong...open the door. You're sick, come on I'm taking you to the hospital," Brick said standing outside of the door. Seriously concerned he tried the knob again. "Baby, open the door. What's wrong with you?" he asked.

"Go away, Brick. I'm ok it must have been something I ate last night...no need for a hospital. I'll be alright," she said slumped over the toilet. She flushed then stood up to look into the mirror. She looked like shit and she felt like it, too. Her face was slightly swollen, her nose had seemed to be a bit too fat. She washed her face and pulled her hair back into a ponytail, Brick knocked on the door.

"Resha, I love you. Would you please open the door? I'm turning into the tin man out here...I need oil."

Resha chuckled and opened the door. For some reason she had appeared more beautiful, he just couldn't put his finger on it. She seemed to glow. He grabbed her and pulled her close to him, hugging her like they had been apart for years. Even after vomiting she smelled like roses. Maybe she was the one, who knows.

"One of these days I'm going to marry you," he said not knowing exactly where that came from. It just felt like the right thing to say. She leaned back and glanced into his eyes.

"Do you mean it?" she whispered softly.

"Of course I mean it, just wait and see...the big house, white picket fence....the whole nine, just wait."

"Wait for what? Life doesn't wait. I want to be with you always."

"And you will be," Brick said. "I just have to get things right financially then it's me and you, smooth sailing with sand between our toes." Somewhere inside he probably meant it, but the guilt was overwhelming. Just a few hours ago he was boning a stripper doggy style in a Jacuzzi and now he was talking about marriage.   Be   for   real.

Justus set the south side on fire, quarters, halves and wholes. He was eating the competition alive. Hell you could even buy a single if you purchase two. The hundred birds that he had received, he had stretched courtesy of Junky Pookie. Not too much, one hundred plus fifty, just enough to keep them coming back. In two days he had already met his quota and J.C. Napier was starting to look like New Jack City. The feins were lined up outside the trap all day long. Some sleeping in hallways, his workers sold double ups, twenty dollars could buy you a gram. There was so much traffic he rented two more apartments. At first other dealers were against his take over, but his prices were so cheap that eventually they gave in. They didn't know much about Justus besides he stayed strapped and ran the smoothest operation they had ever seen.

Lately he had been pushing a black Range Rover, the nigga had style no doubt about that. He would give almost anybody a chance to get some money, that's how he met T.J. T.J was a hot boy fresh out of prison after doing a dime. He hadn't been out a month and was already on the grind. He felt like the world owed him something and he definitely wanted it. He had come to Justus with all he owned: a thousand dollars and a desire to get paid. He left with a thousand dollars, a phone number, one key and a Tec 9. Now employed by Justus, he was dying to show his loyalty. No one had ever treated him as good as Justus. Everything that he had ever gotten he had worked for it, even in prison. Nobody sent him a dime, he was forced to rob niggas and gamble and of course gambling always led to more robbery because he was a sore loser. He was Justus' ears to the streets; nothing happened on the south side that he wasn't aware of. They sat on the steps of the projects shooting the breeze.

"Naw for real fool, I was going to smoke Gay Gay ass about that lil paper until you told me that it wasn't worth it...I need that little bit, punk ass nigga got a death wish," T.J said twisting up a stick of high dro. At a distance cops rode bicycles through a bridge way, everyday routine in the hood. Their presence scared no one. People here were immune to the police. Guns still clapped and the crack was still being sold.

"You'd be a damn fool. Let that nigga play himself. Look at it this way, you bought that nigga for an ounce now you ain't got to worry about him asking for nothing else...kill him with silence, eventually he'll come to you because he don't know what's on your mind. One things for sure, TJ and you can bet your last on this...niggas know who they owe. They might pretend like they done forgot and shit...aw! Look out!"

"BOOM!" suddenly gun fire erupted as Gay Gay stepped from behind a building with a sawed off shotgun aimed straight at TJ blasting. The sawed off lit the hallway up like the sky on New Years Eve. TJ stood up to run, but was hit in the back causing him to collapse immediately. Gay Gay turned to run, but met a hell of Justus' bullets. His 40 caliber breathed fire like a dragon striking Gay Gay in the back of his upper torso. His arm went limp immediately dropping the gage. He disappeared near the bridge-way leaving a trail of blood. Justus decided not to chase him. TJ was dying and needed help. He had managed to turn over on his back and there was a hole the size of a grape fruit in his stomach. The slug had gone clean through. He was bleeding and his eyes were rolling in the back of his head. Justus kneeled down and placed his hand under TJ's head. He was in bad shape and still trying to talk.

"I, I, I told you," he said as his soul left his body departing to the next world eyes staring up at the sky. Gay Gay had paid him alright, paid him in bullets. It was then that Justus learned that some rules just don't apply to some niggas, some niggas got to be killed ASAP.

The gun shot blast seemed to cause an earthquake echoing from miles and felt by everybody in the room, for a minute there was silence.

"Damn Dog, sounds like somebody done got flipped...listen nigga you hear that," Tony said strolling through the living room of the small apartment gripping a sub machine gun. He peeked out the window and looked up and down the street for any signs of commotion and then there it was, a scream, kind of distant but still close enough to be heard. Suddenly a small shadow darted past the window. Tony jumped, caught off guard by the swift moving shadow.

"What the hell is going on out there?" Quack said quickly rising up off the couch and joining Tony at the window.

"I think some nigga done got shot up down there in the cut it's blood all in the hall...I see some people running and it's broad day light outside. These niggas crazy, the police finna be hotter than a fire cracker around this piece. Call Justus and tell him that we finna shut this shit down," Tony said. Tony was twenty two but no fool. Although he didn't complete high school he was book and street smart.

"I was thinking the same thing" Quack said dialing Justus' number. No answer so he tried back.

"Hello?"

"Bruh this Q. We 'bout to shut it down. Some niggas clapping outside. I think somebody done got hit, I can hear the ambulance now. Where you at?"

Justus paused as if trying to collect his thoughts.

"Bruh," Quack said.

"Yea, yea I'm here."

"Where's here?"

"On my way to pick up Brick. That was me you heard, Gay Gay just killed T.J, I hit him up but he got away...hey let me call you right back. I need to check something".

Brick was posted in University Court a block over from Justus. The projects were the same, but the money was too slow. He had hardly sold any coke which had put him in a state of depression. He had four days left to get off a hundred bricks and he had only sold two. Maybe this heavy weight shit wasn't for him. Lately he had been partying with a couple of hood rats that he had met the other day. In search of weed and white, they knocked on his door and never left. All they wanted to do was get high and swallow cum. He'd take turns fucking them both in the ass, they were true sluts with no limits, willing to do anything for a blunt and a hit of powder. Sherry and Mary were the ultimate evils. Somehow they had convinced him to take a snort. Maybe that's why he couldn't make any money. All that he seemed to want to do now was get high and freak, he was turning into a slouch. The house was a complete wreck, empty patron bottles and trash littered the floor he hadn't eaten in two days. If Justus found out that he was using it would be the end of their friendship for sure. Justus didn't play that junky shit and Brick knew it. He had seen it kill his auntie. Sometimes he even suspected Pam was using he just never could prove it.

There was a knock at the door. Brick got up and looked out the peephole. "Shit!" It was Justus. Something had to be wrong, he hadn't even called first. Brick wiped his face with his shirt double checking his nose before opening the door. Justus walked pass Brick and took a seat on the couch. He scanned the living room briefly and then stopped eyes resting on the two hoes asleep on the floor.

"What the fuck you been doing and who are these tired ass bitches? This is how you live now? This house smells like shit."

Brick frowned and retorted, "Hell naw this ain't how I live. I had a party last night. I just got up not too long ago...my cleaning lady ain't been by yet," Brick said.

"When the last time you've been home? I talked to Resha this morning and she said that she hadn't heard from you nor seen you. She's worried, you need to call her," Justus said.

"I was there the other day. I was supposed to go back, but something came up at the spot," Brick said.

"Man, you need to get yourself together. You look bad dog." Justus shook his head back and forth. "You don't seem like yourself," Justus said. Deep inside Brick knew he was right and the last thing that he wanted to do was make Justus mad so he remained quiet taking it all in.

"Guess what just happend?" Justus said with a look of seriousness on his face.

"What you won the lottery?" Brick said jokingly.

"Not quite…no need. Actually yesterday I made my first million funny ass nigga, no lie. I counted that shit until my hands hurt then threw the rest in the closet," he said with a hint of sarcasm in his voice. Brick knew Justus was serious, he'd always been the better hustler, he envied him.

"I wish that I could say the same thing, but shits been slow on my end…maybe you're making all the money.." Brick laughed, Justus didn't crack a smile.

"T.J got killed. That nigga Gay Gay got the ups on us. I lit his ass up but he got away…T.J died in my arms, man. I still hear him in my head saying 'I told you so'. I should have let him kill that nigga when he wanted to."

Brick stared with an unbelievable look of shock on his face.

"Well it's on now, his ass bound to pop up and when he do, we'll flat line his ass. Until then we'll just keep our ears to the streets."

Sherry woke up and was listening to the conversation with her eyebrows raised high, "Damn that's messed up about T.J. I ain't trying to get in y'all business or nothing, but I use to mess with Gay Gay. His dirty ass stays with Jody, his baby momma in Hillside. I know because that's where I threw his clothes out at when I caught him cheating...when you catch him give him one for me," Sherry said drinking the last corner of Patron from the bottle.

"Ay Brick let me holla at you in the kitchen," Justus said making his way through the living room. Brick followed, he glanced back mean mugging Sherry. As soon as they stepped through the door Justus started, "Man you've got these scandalous ass hoes out here ease dropping trying to set a nigga up." Justus pointed his finger in Brick's face. "The same way that they put us on the next nigga, they'll put the next nigga on us...wake the fuck up this ain't no lil boy shit no more. A nigga will blow your fucking top off 'bout them bricks. It's on you, do what you want, but leave me out of it!" Justus turned and walked out the kitchen. When he left the apartment he left the door standing wide open.

Brick could tell that he was pissed. He had to get his self together. He shut the door and locked it. First he had to get his head together. He sat down placing an ounce of powder on the table. Mary fetched the plate, they smiled greedily...

CHAPTER 18

FAVOR FOR A FAVOR!!!

"Meet me at the Mall in Rivergate...I'm leaving Hendersonville now. I should be there in twenty minutes, come by yourself," Low said into his blackberry, knees steering the wheel and a fat blunt in his hand.

Justus was in Madison, ten minutes from the Mall. The meeting place was perfect. Justus could shop at the same time. Low was a couple of days early for the drop, his call was unexpected. He hadn't talked to him since the first meeting. Good thing he was done early, he thought to himself. He had planned to call him in about an hour anyway. His intentions were to surprise him with how fast he worked. He had stacked two million cash in hundreds and fifties neatly in the back of his black Range Rover. Not only was he about to pay for the hundred that he was fronted, he was also about to buy a hundred, too. Even Low would have to admit that he was on top of his game. Justus smiled to himself while pulling into the Mall parking lot. Five minutes later, Low arrived in a gray Audi Z. He beeped his horn signaling for Justus to follow. Justus trailed him to the back entrance of the Mall facing the interstate. He parked then got out all smiles.

Low was dressed in a gray and blue Miskeen jogging suit and matching timberlands, his gear complemented the Audi. He walked like he had been a boss all of his life, use to power, sure of himself, no insecurities, all the things that made great leaders. He approached the back of his Audi and sat on the trunk searching the parking lot for cameras, Justus approached.

"I hit you up a little early, something came up...I'm sure you wanted to see me, I hope I didn't inconvenience you," Low said.

"Of course not. Hell I was about to hit you up anyway. Consider this perfect timing. I've got something that I want you to check out in the truck." Justus smiled turning around headed for the Rover. Low swaggered over.

"Dig man this is a nice whip. I pictured you more of a Mercedes nigga. I had one of these a couple of years ago, I gave it to a shorty for his birthday," Low said.

"I like Mercedes too. Funny you said that, this was my second choice. I almost copped that 600, but I needed a little more room for the bitches," they laughed. Justus opened the back of the Range and there it sat, Mr. Ben Franklin himself.

"It's all there, actually it's two mill...put me in the game coach." Justus searched Low's face for excitement... not a hint. Low was used to money, he was a walking dollar sign. He had warehouses of the shit. Low closed the trunk himself.

"Well, well. I see you're a man of many surprises, my type of cat...if I didn't know any better I would say that you're trying to impress me, mind you I don't impress easily, but this is good." Low went on to tell a story, "Once while I was visiting Paris I had misplaced my luggage, I was staying at the Better Sweets, have you ever been to Paris?" Low asked. Justus shook his head no.

"Well, anyway, nice place you should go sometimes, the city of love. I had misplaced my luggage and in one of my briefcases was a mill in cash. All of a sudden there was a knock at my room door. When I opened it to my surprise it was the valet returning my bread. He insisted that he wanted no reward and told me to have a nice trip. When he was leaving I told him that being broke impresses no one, I rather he kept it than park cars all his life, but who am I to judge. I have a surprise for you also," Low said walking back to the car. "It isn't as great as yours, but it's nice never the less." Low pushed a button on his keychain and his trunk automatically began to rise. Justus' face twisted in shock he couldn't believe it, it couldn't be true, but it was as real as the sun.

Justus' look of shock twisted into an evil grin. There in the trunk of Low's Audi ducked taped, gagged and hog tied was Gay Gay with a look of terror on his face. Justus tried to speak but stuttered.

"Ho...ho... how did you know?"

Low tossed his head back in a laugh.

"Nigga I run these streets you haven't figured that out yet? Ain't shit poppin' off that I ain't aware of. Call it a favor for a favor." Suddenly Low produced a glock 45 with a silencer from his waist band placing it on the temple of Gay Gay's head and fired. The shot was so muffled it sounded as if someone had snapped their fingers. Blood oozed down his face. From the looks of it Low had planned this all along. The trunk was wrapped in plastic although Justus would had loved to have been the one to put the bullet in Gay Gay's head. He was more than satisfied, who didn't want a friend like Low, he was as real as they came. Low concealed the glock and closed the trunk.

"Now time for some shopping," Low said dusting his hands off like he had just did some heavy lifting.

"What about the body?" Justus asked.

Low grinned. "Never mind the trash, somebody, should be here in a minute to take out the garbage…when I leave the mall this car will be replaced by a black one. Who said crime didn't pay?" Low joked.

"Damn straight," Justus said.

River Gate Mall on Fridays kind of reminded you of Mardi Graz or the BET awards. Everybody seemed to be trying to impress somebody, platinum and diamonds, draped the necks and wrists of ballers, tights and skin, broads parading in packs and cats following like hounds.

"This here is one of my favorite stores," Low said pointing at Mafioso's. When they entered they were greeted by an Iranian who knew Low by name. As a matter of fact, he locked the door and turned over the 'out for lunch' sign so Low could shop in private. He loved Low's business, whenever he was in the store he was the only costumer that mattered. He'd spend thousands in minutes and never ask how much anything costs; he was addicted to nice shit.

Justus browsed through the jeans section. There were jeans starting at two grand. The owner assisted Justus.

"This here is the finest of Prince Mane today, on sale just for you. Two pair for five thousand, my deal…great bargain." Although his English was broken Justus understood him perfectly. Was he serious? Justus thought it was no way in hell he'd spend five grand on two pair of jeans, hell he could shop at Hang Time and get ten pair for that price.

"No thank you. I'm just looking," said Justus.

"Aww come on man. Looking is for broke niggas, broke nigga outside of store, you're with the Don…show me the money," he said in his foreign accent a polite smile graced his face. Low interrupted.

"Hey Tyreke get me four of these in a thirty six and a few pair of boots to match, alligator preferably," Low said.

"No problem. I got just the thing," Tyreke said heading for the back of the store where he kept his VIP selection. Most people couldn't afford the items kept back there so there was no need to display them. Tyreke even dealt in diamonds. For the right price he could produce stones as big as marbles. He returned with Low's order neatly wrapped and placed it on the counter. Low peeped inside, after seeing one pair of boots he immediately said, "Double this order up for my boy, same deal...Yo Jay what sizes do you wear?"

Justus was busy looking at a hat amazed that even the hat was a thousand dollars.

"Aww dog you ain't got to do that, I'm straight."

"I know that I ain't got to do shit. Consider it a gift, don't be rude and Tyreke throw that hat in, too." Tyreke hurried over and snatched the hat down that had captured Justus' attention, a big smile on his face as if to say, "I told you so". By the time they had left the store, Low had spent forty three thousand and could carry his bags in one hand. Justus decided to loosen up a bit. Since he was rich now what harm could it do if he splurged a little?

"Boy if Tiffany could see him now." Their relationship was long over. He decided to cut her loose so that she could focus on school and that way he'd have more time to focus on the streets. He put all his energy into his grind. Living alone wasn't so bad. His condo was decked out; he had an elevator built personally for his cat so that he could let himself in and out of the house at will, it was equipped with special censers, that way no unwanted raccoons could hitch a ride. He thought briefly about Brick. Lately he seemed to be off his square, money seemed to be changing him for the worse. They hadn't even been hanging tight recently and poor Resha had stuck by his side during his incarceration now she was barely even seeing him. Justus felt sorry for Resha. She was a good woman and good women were for good men. Somehow she had gotten stuck with Brick. His thoughts were interrupted.

"Hey dog, Cash going to get at you later about that bread, when he calls you just be ready...I suggest you expand your safe house. This next load gone break the scale," Justus nodded. Just then a tall guy in dark black shades walked directly into Low causing him to lose his balance, stumbling but not falling. Justus sprang into action immediately. "Nigga you better watch where the fuck you're going I'd hate to make you eat those big ass glasses...you owe my man an apology." The guy raised his shades and looked around as to say "Are you talking to me?"

"Chill I got this," Low said. "Aw my man didn't mean no harm...excuse us. Have a nice day." The guy smiled as if he had won a prize then turned and walked off never really realizing how close he had just came to death.

"Some things go best unsaid...I consider myself a man of action. Sure I could have killed him right then and been on the news in twenty minutes, but for what when I can kill him later and get away with it. Everything in its proper time, you see Jay look over there." Low nodded his head in the direction of two guys that seemed to be watching him and Justus, one of them left and began to follow the fool in glasses. Justus had never seemed to notice them before and they were being followed the whole time. They were Low's guys, somebody was in trouble.

"You see Jay every fool has his day," Low said.

Two weeks later Justus was sitting on five hundred bricks strong. Things had been running pretty smoothly. He and Low had become pretty tight, he had even traveled to Arizona with Low on business and met some people that Low called family but were clearly Columbians. They ate at nice restaurants and flew nothing but first class. Brick on the other hand was struggling so Justus had to front him the cash to pay Low. When it came time to settle up, Justus was the one moving Brick's supply. After all they were friends and he couldn't stand to see anything happen to Brick. He didn't mind helping him out here and there, of course Brick knew that. That was one of the reasons he partied so hard. This one night he laid stretched out butt naked in a Comfort Inn Hotel on his back with Sherry snorting lines of coke off his stomach. Occasionally she'd suck his balls and talk dirty to him, something he really enjoyed. She ate dick like a hotdog champion in an all you can eat contest. She would wrap her sexy hands around his shaft and masturbate him at the same time causing every one of his toes to curl. Her lips were as soft as cotton and her mouth was as warm as her ass, he was in love with her throat, she was his personal head doctor. He watched her as she walked naked through the room.

"I got to make some money," Brick said to no one in particular thinking out loud. He wiped the sweat from his forehead and took a swallow of Hennessey.

"If you want me to I can make some calls...baby. I know several niggas who be buying weight. Maybe I could turn you on to them," Sherry said flopping down on the bed next to Brick.

"Like who? Them project ass niggas ain't got no money. I'm talking 'bout some serious stacks," Brick said looking out the window from the sixth floor staring into space.

"My boy Kool-Aid be moving weight out in Woodbine and I ain't talking 'bout no little shit either...I can check with him," she said digging in her purse for her cell phone.

"Why you ain't been done said nothing? I got plenty of shit that I need to move." Brick picked up the plate from off the night stand and snorted a line. He felt the coke rush to his brain. His nose began to drain. "Hit that nigga up...see what's up."

Sherry scrolled through her call log, finding his number she pressed send.

"Time is money," a voice answered.

"Kool-Aid it's me Sherry. What it do?"

"You tell me. Where you at? I've been needing to holla at you anyway, we still got unfinished business...I was too high last time, but I'm ready now."

"Boy you crazy that ain't the reason why I'm calling you...I'm calling you for my ol' man."

Kool-Aid laughed. "Ol' man, ain't no nigga stupid enough to call you his woman."

"Nigga what you tryin' to say?"

"Nothing, I said it."

"Anyway, he wants to know if you're interested in buying something."

"Like what? I don't need no hot shit, and I already got more straps than I can count…what is it that he's trying to get rid of, you?" Kool-Aid asked.

"Whatever nigga."

"I really can't say it on the phone, but I'm sure you want it."

"Aww yea, how sure?" he said.

"Absolutely sure it's a deal. So good you can't refuse," Sherry said.

"Aww I see, must be nice."

"Let's put it this way, you know that shit Tony Montana got from Solsa?"

Kool-Aid paused, "Yea. Hell yea. I'm following you."

"Good, it's that. A lot of it," she said.

"How much is a lot?"

"How much do you need? He can get what ever you need and never run out."

"Aww I see…sounds good. How soon?"

"Like right now soon, pull up at your front door and drop it off soon."

How much we talking, what's the ticket?"

"For what?"

"For all of it."

Sherry covered the phone and whispered to Brick, "How much is the ticket?"

Brick took another snort. "Tell him seventeen a piece, fifty or better fifteen."

Sherry removed her hand from covering the receiver, "Eight teen apiece fifty or more sixteen."

Brick frowned, "That ain't what I said."

Sherry corrected herself disappointed he wouldn't allow her to make anything.

"Sounds good, check this out I'm finna count my bread. I'ma call you back at this number in two minutes alright?" Kool-Aid said.

"Don't have me waiting, there's plenty of other niggas who want this shit," Sherry said.

"I know baby...two minutes that's it." And the line went dead.

Two minutes later Kool-Aid called back. Sherry answered it on the first ring.

"Hello?"

"Yea it's me again…look I need fifty of them all brick, no shake."

"Nigga please my nigga name is Brick. What that tell you?"

"Tells me that he's stupid. Nobody with sense would name himself something like that."

"What the hell ever. Nigga you got the money?"

"Hell yea I got the money, that's why you called. You know that I got the money," Kool-Aid replied.

"You're damn straight, when you want it?" she asked.

"I want it now. Where do I need to come?"

"Hold on for a minute." She covered the phone, "Baby, he said he want fifty where do he need to come?" Brick looked shocked, he couldn't believe that this bitch had just sold fifty birds and he could hardly sell ten in a good week.

"Tell him to meet me in JC in twenty minutes. Give him the address."

Sherry gave Kool-Aid the address. Ten minutes later her and Brick were at the spot getting the order. Brick stuffed twenty five in each duffle bag neatly, Sherry watched.

"Damn! That's a lot of coke. I didn't know that you had that much really and you keep it all in here."

"Naw I don't keep it all in here all the time and yes this is a lot of coke. I ain't gone play about my money either so I hope your boy straight...you see this?" Brick removed a Tec9 from one of the bags. "It's real."

"Boy he ain't stupid and he ain't on no shit like that." Suddenly there was a knock at the door. Brick looked out the peep hole.

"Aww shit it's the police," he ran into the kitchen and attempted to hide the dope. Sherry looked out the peep hole as the knocking continued.

"Boy that ain't the police, that's Kool-Aid. You're crazy," Sherry laughed. Brick came out of the kitchen sweating. "You didn't tell me that he was a white boy."

"What does it matter if he can pay what he weigh?" she said.

"I ain't never served no white boy and when have you ever seen one in these projects?" Brick asked.

"Are you going to open the door and make this money or what?"

Brick opened the door and Kool-Aid came in. He was carrying a small tote bag.

"What's up my man? My name is Kool-Aid as you may have heard." He extended his arm to shake Bricks hand. For a minute Brick was caught off guard then he shook it. "My name is Brick."

"Hell of a name," Kool-Aid joked.

"So is 'Kool-Aid', but let's get down to business. Sherry tells me that you're good peoples," Brick said.

"I'd like to think of myself as such...I don't start no shit and I get money so I guess you can say I'm ok to be around."

Brick smiled. Kool-Aid noticed the Tec in Brick's hand.

"No need for guns my man. I'm just here for product, no trouble." He placed the tote bag on the table and unhooked the latch.

"Fifteen a piece right? The math is straight you can count it."

Brick picked up a stack of hundred dollar bills and thumbed through it.

"Looks good to me, I'll make a deal with you. If I count this and it ain't proper, I'ma kill you right here and right now." Brick searched Kool-Aid's face for any sign of fear when he seen none he said, "Never mind I trust you," and laughed.

"Good." Kool-Aid said. "This is the start to something beautiful." Brick set the coke on the table.

"Here you go, fifty just like I said." Kool-Aid picked up both bags and threw them over his shoulders.

"You ain't gone count your shit?" Brick asked

"For what I trust you and I hear good things about you. If it ain't right, I'll be back." Kool-Aid smiled and headed for the door. In five minutes he was out of sight. Brick was excited, he couldn't wait to tell Justus about his new white boy. Sherry was excited, too. She texted Mary on her cell phone two words: "Party Time." Mary responded: "I'm on my way."

Brick began to pour the money out on the floor. He had become so aroused he decided that he wanted to fuck Sherry on the money. What could be better than making love on a bed of Ben Franklin's. It was then that he noticed that something was terribly wrong, some of the bundles appeared to be stuffed with green paper. How could he had been so stupid not to have checked each stack? In a rage he ripped open each stack. Almost every single one of them was green paper, a couple of hundreds on top and a couple on bottom. This bitch was dead no doubt about it! He was going to kill him and everybody he loved, but first he would kill Sherry. Like a trained assassin he wrapped both of his hands around her throat and squeezed until she foamed at the mouth, her eyes changed colors.

"Pleeease," she tried to say, but it was no use, Brick was literally strangling her to death. Her feet kicked as he choked her then suddenly she stopped, her body limped in his arms. He continued to squeeze and for a minute he was someone else. He let her lifeless body drop to the floor. What had he done? He knew damn well what he had done, now it was time to find Kool-Aid. He picked up Sherry's phone and he redialed, no answer just the machine, "Yea this is Kool-Aid. If you feel like you've been played get at you're boy, Beep."

Brick left a message. "Mother fucker you have something that belongs to me, I want them fifty back plus interest. You've got twenty four hours then I'm going to burn Woodbine down to the ground." He hung up, it was time to call Justus.

Resha sat at Centennial Medical Center all by herself. It was her first doctor's appointment. They had already run several tests and she was waiting on the results. She was nervous, but it was something that she knew she had to do. When the nurse came back into the room she could tell from the look on her face that it was serious.

"Well Resha we have some good news and some bad news which one do you want first?" Resha was more afraid than ever now. "Did you say bad news?"

"Yes I'm afraid that I did. I hate to be the bearer of bad news, but somebody just has to otherwise things just wouldn't be right." The nurse forced a smile.

"Ok, give me the good news first," Resha said.

"Well the good news is you're pregnant, sixteen weeks to be exact...Congratulations," said the nurse.

Resha didn't budge nor crack a smile.

"The bad news is that you have an STD and if you're not treated immediately it could damage the baby."

Resha broke down and began to sob loudly.

"Now, now it's ok baby you're not dying. I'm just saying that we need to get you a shot and take care of it before it gets too bad...Do you have any idea where you could have gotten this from?" asked the nurse.

Resha felt insulted, she hadn't slept with nothing but two men in her life, one of them being her husband and he was dead the other being Brick. Damn right she knew who gave it to her. That nasty son of a bitch, she could kill him.

"What is it?" she asked the nurse.

"It's Gonorrhea...it's a pretty rough disease, actually it's a wonder you didn't realize that you had it. I guess the discharging hadn't started. It's different for women, but if you were a man you would have known immediately...just wait here I'll get you all fixed up and you'll be ready to go in no time. I'm scheduling you to come back in two weeks." Looking at the calendar, "that would be February the 6th at 7 o'clock..."

CHAPTER 19

KOOL-AID!!!

The dark brown 2012 Chevy Impala pulled up in Riverchase, a gated community on the east side. Kool-Aid decided not to go back to Woodbine after hearing Brick's message. Fuck Woodbine and Brick, too. He was a sucker and had made the lick too easy. He was expecting at least a little gun play, that's why he carried the 380 in the small of his back, but the dumb ass nigga made it too easy talking about "I trust you." Ha,ha ha, he thought to himself. As he parked and got out of his Impala a black Taurus pulled up beside him. The window rolled down and out leaped flames. The Mac showered him like a rain cloud, he was dead before he hit the ground. The passenger of the Ford Taurus got out, taking the keys from Kool-Aid's ignition. He opened the trunk of the Impala retrieving the duffle bags and leaving Kool-Aid in a puddle of blood before speeding off. From a distance it kind of looked like Kool-Aid.

"Bruh you got to help me, this is the honest to God truth. I fucked up big. I'm at the spot man, you gotta swing by," Brick said.

"What the hell's up now?" Justus said into his BlackBerry, he was just about to hop in the shower before Brick called.

"Man, I've been robbed!" Brick screamed through the phone.

"You've been what!...Calm the fuck down. I'm not deaf, I can hear. What you mean you've been robbed?" Justus had one foot in the tub and one foot out.

"Man, the bitch Sherry hooked me up with this white boy name Kool-Aid. He came to the spot to buy 50, the fool hit me with some counterfeit bruh. I'm 'bout to lose my mind. I need you," Brick said.

"That ain't all you're about to lose if you don't come up with that bread nigga. I told you in the beginning don't mess this up by any means, now look at you. You've done just that. I'm tired of covering for your ass. You're not a fucking kid... all I do is lose, lose, lose with you. I'm sick of your shit dog. Consider this a good bye present. I suggest you drop out of the race before you end up dead." Justus had hoped it would never come to that, but in his heart he knew he was right.

"I warned you about them hoes," Justus said.

"I killed her bruh. She's here now, dead, that's what I'm trying to tell you."

"In your spot?! You fucking moron. Look, I'm bringing you 50 tonight, after that lose my number, this is the end of the road. I can't carry you forever. You've gotten too fucking heavy."

One week later the entire family was called for an emergency meeting. No one knew exactly what was going on, but everybody was expecting some heads to roll.

Low looked pissed and Cash hadn't spoken since he had arrived. Everyone seemed to have been in their own separate worlds. Killer sat next to Low, Major sat next to Killer, Eric and Derrick were together as always, Quack was in the middle of the table, Brick and Justus sat beside each other, although they hadn't spoken in a week. Justus kind of felt that maybe this was what the meeting was about, but then again one could never be sure. Low began by reminding everyone of how fortunate they were to be part of the family and asked if anyone had any questions. When no one spoke up, he said, "Envy killed Cain, Foot didn't kill Cain. Cain's own hatred brought about his demise, he felt entitled to something that he was never entitled to. He wanted respect, but didn't do what was necessary to earn it." Low looked around the room at everybody letting his words sink in. "He fucked off a million dollar operation. I won't stand by and watch that happen again. Trust is a must, the fungus that's among us will be eradicated. The only way a man loses 50 bricks is if he lost his fucking mind," Low said.

Brick felt a sharp pain go through his chest, was Low talking about him? If so how did he know? For sure Justus would never betray him. He tried to keep a straight face.

Low continued, "Some of us deserve a pat on the back while others deserve a bullet in the head. For instance Justus here, if there ever was such a thing as a successful business man, this is it...here's your role model. He quadrupled his net worth in a month's time. Next to me he's probably the richest muthafucker in the room...no offense Cash."

"None taken," Cash answered back.

Killer was becoming furious, he hated being put on the spot, especially for a new nigga. Where did Low get off comparing him to Justus? He had been around for years and had his back when it was just the three of them, before the twins even. Now Killer felt as if Low had forgotten all the shit they had been through. Sure it was Low who brought them where they were today, but he played a huge part in it also, at least he felt he did. The truth was he wasn't Low's equal and he knew it, hell he wasn't even close. But he be damned if he sat back and watched Low put that Justus, the new nigga, on a pedestal. Fuck that. His hatred for Justus burned inside like a candle. Someway, somehow he would get rid of him, it was just that simple. He had to go, there was no room for the both of them. With him gone Low would see what an asset he really was then he could appreciate some loyalty. As for now, his judgment was cloudy and it would take him to clear it. He knew what he had to do as soon as the meeting was over. After everybody had been dismissed he made an important phone call.

"Hello?"

"FBI tip hot line."

"Yes, I would like to report a murder," Killer said.

"Who has been killed sir?" the agent responded.

"Well actually it's not one murder, it's a few. They happened in umm… Percy Priest about a few months ago. Some Columbians…do you remember?" Killer asked. The agent typed away on the computer pulling up files.

"Oh yea here it is now. I know exactly what you're talking about and you know who's responsible?" asked the agent.

"Well of course," Killer said.

"How do you know? Were you involved?" the agent asked.

"Let's just say that I was there when the order was given.... hell I was practically an eye witness," Killer said.

"So what's your name?" the FBI agent asked.

"Well, I rather not give you my name, but I'll give you the name of the person who did it. How about that?" Killer said.

"That would be fine sir," the agent said.

"Good, the name is Justus, sometimes he goes by Jay," he said.

"Who gave the orders?" asked the agent.

"That, I can't say. Goodbye for now." Disconnecting the line, Killer was feeling very devious. Boy he had him now, it was just a matter of time then things would go back to normal. Little did he know back at FBI headquarters, his call had been traced. Agent

Foster jotted down the name on the telephone account: Robert Osborne. He ran the name and did a NCI check. Alias name 'Killer', extensive   back ground, more than enough drug convictions. Yes he had a suspect now. All he had to do was locate him and even that would be easy, his address was listed. Last known place of residence was 911 6th Ave., North Salem Town. Killer had some explaining to do.

At four o'clock am the next day he was awakened by the sounds of FBI agents knocking on his door.

"Robert Osborne at this moment you're not under arrest. We do need you, however, to come with us down to the station and answer some questions," said agent Foster.

Killer was still half asleep, "What the hell is going on?" All the commotion had awaken his girlfriend.

"Baby what's going on?" she asked.

"Michelle, go back to sleep. Everything is alright, they just want to take me and ask me some questions. I'll be right back," Killer said.

"Do you want me to call Low?" she asked. That was the last thing that he wanted her to do.

"No baby, don't call anyone. Everythang is ok. I'll be right back. Just go back to sleep. I'll be back before you know it." Killer left in his pajamas on his way to FBI headquarters. He prayed no one spotted him.

The interrogation room was small; one large mirror, tented window in the corner, kind of reminded him of a movie, but in Killer's case a bad dream. He didn't want to hurt Low, all he wanted to do was destroy Justus. Somehow the FBI had found out that he was the one who had made that call last night. How could he have been so stupid? They know everything, he thought to himself. Agent Foster walked in sipping a cup of Starbucks Espresso. He took a seat next to Killer, but said nothing. For a moment he read his body language; Killer was nervous, that he was sure of. He decided to break the ice.

"Mr. Osborne, my name is agent Foster. I have a few questions that I would like to ask you. Do you have any idea why we brought you here?"

Killer tried denial. "Not a clue," he responded. Agent Foster took a deep breath. He was in no mood to play games with a scumbag criminal.

"Look here, you motherfucking scumbag you know exactly why you're here. I could be charging your ass with murder right now so if you want to play go ahead. Fine, make my day. Now you called us we didn't call you…Who did this shit? Was it you or not?" agent Foster asked.

Killer was beginning to sweat under the collar.

"Naw it wasn't me. I've already told y'all who it was so why am I here? You got the wrong man," Killer said.

"As for right now you're not under arrest…however we might need to use you as a witness," said agent Foster.

Killer interrupted, "No fucking way. I can't get on no stand that's a death sentence. I'm afraid you will have to find someone else," said Killer.

"I'm afraid that you don't have a choice Robert. You witnessed it, you know who the killers are and frankly you're running out of options. Now if need be we can place you in witness protection. We have a nice program. Even if you went to jail you would never leave Charles Bass. Or we can fly you on the other side of the world, give you a brand new start.… a new name even. From the looks of your record you could really use that."

"Man you don't understand there're some things you just can't hide from, this is one of them. If I get on the stand my life is over. Nothing could protect me from Low," Killer said. As soon as the name 'Low' left his mouth, he knew he had made a mistake. He felt his heart stop.

"'Low' you say...see that wasn't so hard now was it? Now you just wait right here and I'll be right back." Agent Foster left the room.

Killer banged his head against the table and laid there faced down. He felt like a piece of shit, he never dreamed that he'd rat out his own family, but there he was blurting out names like the fucking snitch he was. Five minutes later agent Foster walked in with another agent.

"Mr. Osborne my name is Agent West. I would like to ask you a few questions also." He was carrying a folder. When they sat at the table he opened it and spread its contents on the table. There were several shots; one of them showed Cash, Justus and Brick eating at PF Changs, another showed Low and Justus boarding a jet. Where had I been that day? Probably somewhere doing the dirty work, he thought. That picture pissed him off. There were also shots of the twins at LP Stadium watching the Titans game.

Agent West seemed to have been building a case all alone.

"Look, I want you to point out Justus in these pictures. We have reasons to believe that he's one of the guys here...we already know who Low is. He's been on our radar for some time now," the agent said.

Killer shifted in his seat weighing his options.

"That's him," he said pointing at the picture of Justus boarding the jet. He could feel that fire burning inside him once again.

"Are you sure?" asked agent West.

"Who is this other guy?" agent Foster asked pointing to Brick.

"Uhh, his name is Brick, he's a nobody...Justus' side kick," Killer said.

"Was he involved in the murders also?" asked agent Foster.

Killer pondered, "Naw I just seen Justus for sure."

"Where were you?" asked agent West.

"You can say that I was just passing through."

"You did a great service to your country by calling us Mr. Osborne. This is a case that we desperately needed to wrap up. These guys are animals, now with your help we will be able to put these creeps behind bars where they belong. Here's my card. Feel free to contact me whenever you want. If we have anything further we know how to find you. You're free to go, have a nice day. Agent Foster will take you home," said agent West.

"Thanks, but no thanks. I got it from here… just let me use the phone and I'll call a ride."

CHAPTER 20

WHAT GOES ON IN THE DARK!!!

Agent West laughed.

"Hello?"

"What's up buddy? Long time, no hear."

"Hey Tom. How's it going man? I've been busy."

"How was the trip?"

"Aww it was lovely. Who would ever dream Australia was so nice. I want to thank you again for those tickets man, my wife loved it."

"No problem man, anytime. You know as a matter of fact I know how much you love them Yankee's…I got you season passes."

"Aww man, you shouldn't have. How can I ever repay you?"

"Stop it Tom you know you do more than enough. How can I ever repay you?" They shared a laugh.

"Hey look I was calling you with something that you might consider useful. When can we meet?" agent West asked.

"Today, tonight, tomorrow, now is fine," Low said.

"Are you sure you're not busy?"

"Naw I'm not busy. As a matter of fact, I was on my way to the coffee house. If it's not out of your way why don't you meet me there?"

"Sounds great, how long?"

"Fifteen… twenty minutes."

"I'll be there."

"See you soon buddy."

Fifteen minutes later Agent Tom West entered the coffee house on West End Avenue to find Low Don already waiting patiently. He had ordered West his favorite, cappuccino. They shook hands then took a seat.

"What seems to be the problem?" Low asked sipping his espresso. Tom glanced around and lowered his voice. Even though there was no one seated at the table next to them, you just never could be too safe.

"Today we brought a guy in who made an anonymous tip last night. He had information about the murders of the Columbians at the Percy Priest. He identified Justus as the shooter, but don't worry I took care of everything. He mentioned your name also. I showed him a few pictures, you know the ones we did just for the loyalty test," agent West said.

Low nodded.

"He couldn't stop pointing. I hate to be the one to tell you this, but Killer is a rat. Luckily I wasn't off that day. He could have caused some real problems. When I heard that he had information on the Percy Priest case, I made sure that I was the one interrogating him," he said.

Low exhaled. The news was shocking, he never expected Killer to be a snitch. Some niggas you think you know only to find out that you don't know shit. Low shook his head. Tom was risking everything by giving Low this information, but it wasn't the first time. He always kept Low posted with new developments inside the bureau. They were old high school buddies, although their life styles were worlds apart, they remained friends to the end.

"Well it is what it is. I'll take care of it...thanks a lot Tom," he said tossing the rest of his espresso in the trash. There was work to be done.

"No problem, anytime. And again thanks for Australia, we had a blast," Tom said.

"Aww, I almost forgot," Low said digging into his jacket pocket. He removed a white envelope and slipped it across the table. "These are those passes that I was telling you about."

"This is a little fat for some passes," Tom said picking the envelope up and peeking inside.

"Oh yea, it's ten grand, too. What's a Yankee's game without popcorn," Low said. Tom smiled sticking the envelope into the pockets of his trousers. He stood up to embrace Low. It had been years since he had hugged another man, but Low had that effect on people.

"I love you man," Tom said.

Brick staggered into the bathroom of the trap house after downing shot after shot of Tequila. He was drunk as a skunk. On top of the liquor he had snorted about a quarter ounce of powder by himself. He missed Sherry's company, but Mary was just as wild. He had convinced Mary that Sherry had flown to Miami on business for him at the last minute. That way she wouldn't keep asking where she was. Truthfully she was at the bottom of the Cumberland feeding the fish, the same place Kool-Aid was going to be if he caught up with him. Briefly he thought about the 50 bricks he had lost. If Justus hadn't saved him he'd also be at the bottom of the Cumberland. One hand on the wall, he held himself up and unzipped his pants waiting for the piss to flow. Suddenly pain ripped through his penis followed by a fountain of blood followed by a scream, his shit was on fire! It felt like he was pissing flames. He grabbed the head and attempted to stop the flow as he peed all over the wall and the floor.

"Are you alright in there?" Mary's voice came from outside the door.

"Yea just fine, be out in a minute," suddenly Resha flashed in his mind. It was like De ja vu; Resha inside the bathroom, him on the outside. He needed to call her, it had been so long since he heard her voice. No, better yet, he needed to go home. That's if he still had a home. She probably had thrown his clothes out by now, but he hoped not. There was only one way to find out, but first he had to find out what was wrong with his dick. He sobered up from all the pain. Next stop Vanderbilt hospital.

Low invited Justus out to his house to discuss business. It was the safest place he could imagine; tucked away nicely in the woods, surrounded by acres of beautiful land, two man-made ponds: one housed piranhas and the other baby alligators. Justus was one of the very few people to ever see this place. Built plantation style, 11 bedrooms, 6 baths and a adjoining guest house in the back, although no guest ever stayed there, Low used it for his counting room. Expensive sports cars filled the 6 car garage. It was truly a peaceful place to escape to. They talked on the patio.

"You know sometimes I wish that I was a bird," Low said looking out into the trees surrounding his property. "They have no worries...in the mornings they wake with nothing and set out in search of God's grace and by evening they return full with plenty to spare for their young. A bird hardly ever starves to death, their nest is never raided by police and the beach is always just a flap away."

Justus understood clearly what he was saying. At times he felt the same way.

"Baby, would you like something to drink?" Low's girl, Debbie, the chocolate stallion he'd warned everybody about, asked from behind the screen door. "I just made fresh lemonade," she said.

"No thank you, baby. Not now, maybe later. How 'bout you Justus?" Low looked at Justus.

"No thank you. I'm good for now," Justus said.

"Just holler if you change your mind," she winked and strolled off. She had the ass of a mule. She was nice to look at, but definitely off limits.

"I have some bad news," Low said still starring out into the woods. Justus could tell that whatever it was, was weighing heavily on Low's mind. He looked like he hadn't slept in days.

"What is it?" Justus asked. Low turned to face him.

"Man, I never thought that I'd say this, but Killer is 5-0," Low said. Justus took a deep breath, his eyes wide in shock. Low nodded.

"What do you mean 5-0? 5-0 as in police?" Justus asked.

"I mean 5-0 as in rat ass snitch working for the FBI. Pointing fingers, dropping names....ours in particular," Low said. This was too much at one time for Justus to digest. His head began to swim so he took a seat in the patio chair. Low remained standing.

"So what are you going to do?" Justus asked.

"It ain't what I'm going to do, it's what you gonna do. I'm afraid this is so personal that I'll become messy, but for you it's just business. Therefore you'll keep a clear head, which is needed. I'm no fucking fool. Emotions will get your ass killed or a hundred years. This got to stay business," Low said.

"Say no more. It's done," Justus interrupted. A minute passed in silence.

"And Justus don't underestimate this fool. If he can go feds ain't no telling what he's capable of...waste no time."

"Let's get it." Justus turned to leave with murder on his mind. If Killer was talking to the feds, there was no time to waste.

"Jay," Low called. Justus turned around. "Don't you want to ask me how I know?" he asked.

"Of course not, your word is good enough for me. If you believe it, that's all that matters...I trust you." Justus meant every word and Low knew it too. He had an eye for sincerity. He smiled. Justus jumped into his Range Rover and sped off to go pay Killer a visit...

CHAPTER 21

MAILMAN!!!

Resha had been so sick lately that she had been calling in from work. Whatever she tried to eat seemed to come right back up. There was no way she could work under these conditions. On top of this, she had been depressed. She had received a voicemail from Brick promising to come by, but so far he was a no show and when she tried calling him it was no answer. It was a good thing, too. Boy did she have a lot of shit to say! Her brother had been coming by to check on her every day, seeing him made her feel so much better. He was really all she had and she didn't blame him for being so over protective, especially now. She understood what he had been doing all along; trying to protect her from no good ass niggas like Brick, but no, she had to be 'Miss Hard-Head.' Now look at me, she thought. Her job was the farthest thing from her mind since she was in no need of money. Somehow every Friday when she went to check the mailbox there was a ton of cash, no less than ten thousand every time. For the past month or so this had been happening. She had even tried to catch who was doing it, but to no avail. So she had given up trying. She was just grateful that it was there. So far she had saved every dime totaling eighty one thousand. That was a good start. The baby would have everything it needed. She thought about Brick, wondering where he was and if he was thinking about her. Probably not, she cried.

Salem Town was where all the hopeless people went when they had given up on life. Trash filled the yards, torn plastic bags, broken glass. Not a building was free from the cans of paint the local gangs used to tag their territory. A natural gloom seemed to set over the neighborhood, one that couldn't be missed. Today there wasn't a soul outside, not a kid in the street, not a crack head in an alley way. Justus pulled in Killer's driveway next to an old beat up El Camino with bullet holes front to back. From the looks of it someone was trying to kill the owner. Justus got out and adjusted the glock on his hip. He climbed the steps and tapped on the door a few times covering the peep hole with his finger. He could hear the latch being unhooked before the voice said, "Who is it?"

"Me," he said as the door slowly opened. There stood Chelle, Killer's ole lady, a sorry excuse for a woman. Every nigga in Salem town had slept with her. She had been fucking since she was a kid. What made Killer take her as his girl was a mystery. She was clearly a free loader that leached off of whoever she could.

"Is Killer home?" Justus asked.

"Yea he's back there playing that damn game, come on in Jay," she said. Justus walked straight past her and headed for Killer's room. The door was unlocked, so Justus let himself in.

"Baby, give me one of them popsicles out of the freezer," Killer said before turning around to see Justus standing in the middle of the floor. The shock caused him to drop the joy stick. His face looked like he'd seen a ghost.

"Justus, what are you doing here?" he asked, eyes searching the bed for his gun.

"Well, that's no way to greet a friend. If I didn't know any better I'd say that you're not happy to see me," Justus said. Killer smiled.

"Naw man it ain't that. You just spooked the hell out of me. I didn't even hear you come in...where's Chelle?" Killer asked.

"She's in the living room watching TV. This is a nice place you got here. You must have spent a fortune on all the gadgets. Looks like you've got every game that has come out since Tetris...if I had time I would smash you in some Madden, but I'm kind of in a hurry. Today is my mother's birthday. I usually go out to her grave and leave her some fresh flowers, it cleanses my soul. It's something I've done every year since she was murdered," Justus said.

"I didn't know that your mom was murdered. What happened?" Killer asked.

"Long story," Justus said.

"Did they ever find who did it?" Killer asked.

"Naw, but I did and in the end it didn't make me feel any better, but it had to be done," said Justus. Killer stood up and stretched. He had become comfortable now seeing that Justus was just visiting.

"I'm sorry to hear that man," Killer said.

"Yea that's life. I tell you what though, since you ain't doing anything, why don't you come with me? I could use some company and ain't nothing like being with family." Justus stroked Killer's ego.

"Well, I guess I could. How long are we going to be out? I've got some business to take care of for Low a little later," Killer said.

"Not long at all. I'll have you back in no time. I already have the flowers in the trunk so it's a straight shot, no stops," Justus said.

"Cool, lets ride," Killer said. Briefly he considered taking his gun, but quickly dismissed the idea. Hell he was going to a graveyard, everybody there was already dead. On the way out of the house Chelle was standing in the kitchen apparently trying to cook something, but was doing a bad job. The eye on the stove was smoking and she was busy fanning it with a towel.

"I'll be back, baby. Got to make a run," Killer said.

"Whatever," Chelle responded.

"When they got in Justus car, Killer asked, "So what brings you this way anyway?"

Justus tried not to act surprised that he would ask such a question.

"Actually I was just passing through. My aunt stays a street over and the road was blocked so I came this way…decided to stop and see if you was home. Now I'm glad I did because I don't think that I could have handled this by myself this year." Justus pretended like he was searching for his keys, he felt his pockets. "Aww damn, I left my keys on your table when I came in. Hold on I'll run and get them…find us something to listen to nigga, it's plenty of shit in them cases," Justus said getting out of the car. He jogged back to Killer's house and walked straight in, the door was standing wide open from when they had left. Chelle was still standing at the stove. She looked up just in time to see Justus slam the barrel of his glock up against her head. Knocking her unconscious she bent over the stove and slid to the floor. Justus picked up a butcher's knife from the counter and slit her throat from ear to ear. The blood oozed quickly. Next he removed a tattoo from her left arm that read 'Killer' with one slit; he stuffed the skin in her mouth. "Eat that bitch," he said.

Chef Ramsey couldn't have cut with better precision. He wiped his finger prints off of the knife then tossed it on to the floor next to her dead body. With not a drop of blood on him he left the house locking the door behind him, closing it with his shirt. If Killer had any sense he would have noticed that there wasn't a flower in the trunk. But what he would have seen was the AK47 on the floor next to a shovel. Killer had put a Jeezy album on; The Resurrection. They rode and listened to the music. Ten minutes later, they arrived at Greenwood Cemetery. The sun was just beginning to set, the reddish glow stretched across the sky as far as the eyes could see. In the distance the birds were chirping, not a soul was in the cemetery at this time of the day. Justus parked.

"Her grave is just over there," he said pointing at some head stones fifty feet from the curve. He got out quickly and opened the back of the truck, Killer followed.

"I'll get these and you get that," he said rising up displaying the AK. He aimed it at Killer's chest. Killer's eyes bucked. He was shaking like a leaf on a tree. His legs had become paralyzed from fear. He tried, but couldn't move.

"Get the shovel bitch," Justus ordered pointing with his head, both hands gripping the AK. "Bitch, get the shovel!" he screamed. Killer began to cry. Bending over, he lifted the shovel.

"Why are you doing this?" he said through tears. Justus pointed with the AK nudging him in his back, forcing him to move his legs. It felt as if he had a thousand pound weight on.

"Please don't kill me Jay. What about Low? Man we're family," he said, tears pouring.

"See that's where you're wrong," Justus said. "The only family that a rat got is mice. Now dig. Right here is fine and if you think you finna be all night, you're wrong...I'll just put a hundred rounds in your head and leave you lying on a headstone, fuck the ground. Your choice!" Justus shouted.

Killer began to pray "Oh God."

Justus interrupted him, "Nigga don't you dare call on God when all of your life you've worshiped Satan. Didn't even believe that God even existed, but now you're about to meet him face to face," said Justus. Killer had become so weak that he could hardly move. The grave was about five feet. Justus could tell that Killer was desperate.

"BOOM!" the 7 6 2 slug penetrated his stomach causing Killer to fall forward straight into the ditch. He yelled from the bottom, trying to climb out. "Please, please! Justus don't do this! I'm sorry I won't testify!"

Justus began to shovel dirt in Killer's face. He screamed trying to stand up to keep the dirt from covering his head, but it was no use. The hole was filling fast, the screaming had stopped and within minutes the grave had filled and poor Killer was buried alive...

CHAPTER 22

FUN WHILE IT LASTED!!!

Two weeks later, Justus was feeling the pressure of the streets. The game was taking a toll on him. He had all the money he had ever dreamed of, but was still unhappy. Nothing seemed to interest him anymore, he was standing at the top and boy was it lonely there. His best friend, the only friend he'd ever known, had fallen victim to the very thing that was supposed to make him rich. This was the life that he chose, if it hadn't been for him Justus would have never met Low or Cash for that matter. May even still been broke, but at least they had each other, now he had nobody. After the incident with Killer, Low had become extremely paranoid. He figured everybody was the police. He switched his whole operation. Now he was directing everybody to Cash, he didn't give a damn who you were. He had changed his number and everything. Nobody was allowed to talk to him directly but Cash. Cash was running the show and Justus felt like an outcast. After all that he had done for Low now he was getting the cold shoulder. After all the money he had made him, all of the blood he had shed. In the end only to be disregarded like someone who couldn't be trusted. He decided he'd had enough and just like that, it was over. He was worth about 50 million. He figured he'd take the rest of his product and cash out. Move to Argentina, enjoy the slopes, meet some woman and settle down. Get married, have some kids and enjoy life.... the rest of it anyway. It was a simple plan, but first he needed to contact Cash and let him know that he was retiring from the game; sure Cash would understand. The streets were too hot. Anyway, nothing lasted forever and it was just a matter of time before something went terribly wrong. He had already dodged one bullet, thank God. Guess it was time to quit no doubt. He picked up his cell phone and called Cash.

"What's popping?" Cash answered.

"What's up dog? I won't waste too much of your time with this. I'm just calling to inform you that I'm finished...I know when enough is enough, I'm out. Tell Low it's love, but when the trust is gone the love is gone, I'm sure he can relate. I've been doing a lot of thinking lately and I just don't see this going the way that I planned but it was nice while it lasted. We made a lot of money together. It ain't like I owe nobody nothing now. So what I'm trying to say is, I'm out," said Justus.

"Just like that, huh?" Cash asked.

"Just like that," Justus replied.

"Alright then, let me get at Low and I'mma get back at you." Cash was furious as he hung up and contacted Low immediately, the conversation was brief.

"Big Don," Cash said.

"Yea," said Low.

"Man, I just got done hollering at Jay. He wanted me to tell you that he's through," said Cash.

"He's what?" Low asked.

"He's through, as in out the game," Cash responded.

Low laughed. "Ha, ha. Damn right he's out the game and then in a box...ain't no such thing as quitting this family, it's 'til death do us part. I thought that I made that clear a long time ago," Low said.

"You did bruh, but niggas are ungrateful and they're only concerned with self. Now that he's rich he figure he don't need us." Cash was adding insult to injury.

"Dig! You tell that nigga that I said suit up because it's finna rain on his trading ass head...naw better yet, don't tell that nigga nothing. What's up with Brick? They came in together," said Low.

"Aww he's still down. He knows his place and he's extremely grateful," Cash said.

"Good, that's what I want to hear. You tell him I said handle that, I don't care how he does it, but I want Justus dead...he has 24 hours after that he dies. If there's no loyalty then there's no love," said Low.

Brick was shocked to hear the news. Cash had delivered it at the spot in U.C. With him were Eric and Derrick, they were all dressed in black. Brick had almost shitted when he opened the door. Seeing it was them and the manner in which they were dressed, it was obvious that someone was finna die. Brick stood in the middle of the living room floor shirtless listening very carefully to every word leaving Cash's mouth.

"I don't give a fuck if that nigga was your blood, he crossed the family. That nigga got to go, simple as that...do we have a problem?" Cash asked waiting for Brick's response, but it didn't take long.

"I don't know man," he said.

"Dig, let me help you understand. With him out the way you become the man at the same time securing Low's favor. The whole south side would be yours, more coke than you could imagine. You've been slow jogging them same bricks for months and now since Justus has been rich, I bet you don't even know where he lives now do you? How 'bout Brent-fucking-Wood...you ever seen that?" asked Cash. The envy in Brick's eyes was unmistakable, his desire to become Justus was overwhelming. Within minutes his love for Justus had turned into hate, he was more than willing to take on the job. Fuck Justus. He had cut him off a long time ago. It was his time to be king.

"I'll do it," he said. Cash smiled and embraced him hugging him tightly.

He whispered in his ear, "You have 24 hours, after that you die," said Cash. They all left the spot leaving Brick alone, he had some serious planning to do. Cash had left Justus' new address, but Brick just couldn't show up there. He hadn't spoken to Justus in weeks, that would be too obvious. For a minute he doubted himself. He considered packing up his bags and leaving town with all Low's dope and never to return, but he quickly dismissed that idea.

"I can handle it," he said to himself. He knew how Justus worked and thought they had been friends for years. There would be no room for mistakes. Justus would never even see it coming.

Justus was at home watching the satellite when he noticed the black Nissan Altima sitting across the street parked facing his house. That was strange, his neighbors didn't own a black car, he thought. The windows were lightly tinted, but he could tell that there was only one person in the car. Maybe it's someone who's lost. Suddenly the car pulled off and headed the opposite way down the street. Justus followed it with his eyes until it was clean out of his sight. Brick guided the black Altima Coup down a side street. That was the house alright, he was sure of it. He knew Justus' taste and the black cat in the window seal was a dead giveaway. Brick turned around at the end of the street and decided to check out the back of the house. If he knew Justus like he thought he did, there would be a spare key under the rug on the back porch. Justus had done that since he was little, it was a habit, being that he was always locking himself out of the house. Brick would just find the key and let himself in, hide and surprise Justus when he came home. He smiled with excitement. He was a fucking genius if he said so himself.

And there it was again, the same damn Altima. This time it was parked in the alley way, someone had made a feeble attempt to hide it behind some bushes. Something was definitely going on. Justus reached in his closet and retrieved the problem solver from the shelf; it was one of many guns there. It was his favorite, the AR15. He attached the 200 round drum magazine just in case he had more guest than he'd realized. Luckily he had let his maid use his Range Rover to run some errands, there were no other cars in the driveway. He turned off all the lights and crouched low behind his bar using the hardwood oak for cover. He waited patiently like a lion ready to devour his prey.

Sure enough the key was where Brick had expected it to be. He inserted it into the key hole and voila! Like magic the door popped open. Brick smiled deviously shutting himself inside and locking the door back. Since he was in the kitchen he decided to look inside of the refrigerator. Maybe he could find a cold beer, maybe even make himself a sandwich. He laughed to himself removing a pack of bologna and cheese from the refrigerator, placing it under his arm. When he turned around, he was starring directly down the barrel of an AR15.

"How nice of you to join me for lunch," Justus said with one hand turning on the light switch. Brick's eyes were on the verge of popping out of his head. Raising his hands he dropped the bologna and cheese on the floor.

"Hey Jay, this ain't what it look like man," said Brick.

"Of course not.... it never is. So tell me you were just wandering through Brentwood, got hungry, parked your car in the bushes and decided to break in my fucking house?" Justus said.

Brick was so nervous he peed in his pants. Piss trickled down his legs onto the floor.

"I don't blame you," Justus said. "You're in big trouble. Tell me, how much did he pay you?" Justus asked angrily.

"I tried to talk him out of it man, but he wouldn't listen to me," Brick said with tears in his eyes. "They were going to kill me," he cried.

"How much did he pay you?" Justus screamed again.

"He gave me nothing, just an order," Brick replied through clenched teeth.

"You were going to kill me for nothing?" Justus said in disbelief. "After all we've been through." Justus closed his eyes. Brick made his move. Charging Justus like an angry bull, knocking him flat on his back and sending the assault rifle sliding across the kitchen floor. He placed both hands around Justus' neck in an attempt to choke the life out of him. Justus swung punching him in the nose, knocking him clean off of him. They both scrambled to their feet, squaring off in the middle of the floor.

"Come on give me what you got," Brick said. During the struggle his glock had become loose from the small of his back and was now stuck under the refrigerator. Justus swung landing a combination of hooks and jabs against Bricks head sending blood squirting. Brick grabbed Justus and attempted to slam him, but Justus was heavier than he thought, that was his mistake. The uppercut landed right on target knocking Brick clean on his ass, he was seeing stars. Justus kicked with his boots, striking him clean in the mouth crushing his front teeth. Brick screamed in pain lying on his back, he breathed heavily. Justus grabbed his AR15 from off the floor.

"You know Brick, I expected more from you. Now there you are lying on your back finna die just like the rest. Don't you feel lucky?" said Justus. Brick remained silent, he was in too much pain to talk.

"You know Brick there's a lesson to be learned here: that is you don't send a crack head to do a killer's job." Justus aimed at Brick's head and squeezed. The burst from the machine gun reconstructed his face. He was dead on impact. By the time Justus got through cleaning up the mess, wrapping the body and dragging it to Brick's car, the maid was back.

"Hey Susie I've got to make a run. I'll be right back. Bleach this kitchen again, I cut my leg and got a little blood on the floor, but I'm fine," Justus said.

"Yes sir, will do," Susie said.

The ride seemed to take forever. Justus rode in complete silence. It took him exactly one hour and forty five minutes to get from Brentwood to Low Don's hideaway. He remembered the way like the back of his hand, although he'd only been there once. He wasn't even sure if Low was there, but one thing was for sure, he was about to find out.

The nerve of some niggas, all he wanted to do was walk away, but no, they had to go and fuck that up. Now because of Low, Brick was dead.

Justus got out of his all black Range Rover and approached the house, AR15 in hand like a soldier. He didn't bother knocking, if Low was watching his surveillance cameras he'd seen him coming and if not he would die like Scarface. Justus slammed his boot up against the door successfully bending the hinges back. He was met by Debbie, Low Don's chocolate stallion, in her hand was a small caliber pistol, she aimed at Justus and fired missing his head by inches, he squeezed: "tat, tat, tat, tat" the blast from the AR15 chopped her in half and shells poured on the floor like change. Justus made his way up stairs slowly checking every room he passed. There was no sign of Low then he spotted it! A back window open, curtains blowing in the breeze. Low had escaped. Justus darted for the window and looked down. No sign of Low.

"Now you didn't think I'd jump, did you?" a voice came from behind. Justus turned around quickly. He raised and squeezed, so did Low. The impact of the machine gun lifted Low clean off his feet slamming him into a wall causing him to release the Desert Eagle from his palm. When the smoke cleared, he sat slumped against the wall, blood running from his mouth, but still alive.

He spoke in a whisper, "Look what you've done."

Justus stood there still clutching the machine gun. "Na' look what you made me do and to think that I ever trusted you...life is truly a bitch and then you die, not me Low!" Justus screamed, even at the door of death Low had too much pride to die like a coward, he smiled.

Justus began to tell a story, "Envy killed Cain, Foot didn't kill Cain. Cain's own hatred brought about his demise. He felt entitled to something that he was never entitled to. He wanted respect, but didn't do what was necessary to earn it. The fungus is among us and must be eradicated," he imitated Low's speech, something that he took to heart a long time ago.

"See Low, there's something you must know...Foot killed my mother, not directly, but it was his order that killed her just like it was your order that would have killed me. Oh, and by the way just in case you was wondering, I killed Brick, too. I killed Darrel too...you remember him don't you? Maybe, maybe not. I killed Brigit, she was Foot's girlfriend. I shot Bobby and I took your dope that Foot gave him. I would have killed Foot, but the police beat me to it. I know you're wondering why I'm telling you all this, I can see it in your eyes that you couldn't care less, but the point I'm trying to make is this...it was destiny that I met you, it was destiny that you die by my hands." Justus squeezed and showered Low with another burst of bullets, his head jerked and his body tilted over onto the floor. Justus wiped the assault rifle down and laid it up against the wall next to Low's dead body, a going away present. Quickly he made his exit. As soon as he stepped foot outside of Low Don's mini mansion, he was surrounded by black suits and assault rifles.

"Hands! hands! Let me see your hands," the agents yelled. There were black vans everywhere. At least ten vehicles in all, FBI as clear as day. Agent Foster led the pack. Justus' hands were raised to the sky.

"Don't make any moves Justus. You're under arrest for the murder of Robert Osborne, the FBI witness. You have no rights, do you understand?" asked the agent. Justus was puzzled. He knew that he had buried Killer alive and they would never find his body. They were merely fishing, they had nothing.

"Where's my lawyer?" Justus asked as they cuffed and escorted him to the back of a waiting van.

"Where's Low?" agent Foster said. "He's under arrest, too, gentlemen!" he hollered to the rest of the agents. "Search this place upside down and inside out. He's here, I've got a feeling…"

Coming soon: The novel, "Inside Out."

ABOUT THE AUTHOR!!!

C. Wellman, AKA Manwell is to urban fiction what crime is to the hood. A former gangster himself with over a decade lost in the system. Originally from Nashville TN, currently he resigns at W.T.S.P in solitary confinement, locked-down but soul free...

www.ingramcontent.com/pod-product-compliance
Lightning Source LLC
Chambersburg PA
CBHW070058260626
47160CB00004B/1248